NURSE OF GREENMEADOW

The Turrets was a vast and brooding mansion, ruled by an autocratic and crippled old lady. Lovely young Judy Jordan went there to be private nurse to the aged owner and remained to become involved in a romantic and dangerous crossfire between her employer's handsome grandson and her dashing stockbroker — rivals alike for the aged lady's money, her house and then for Judy herself . . .

JANE CORBY

NURSE OF GREENMEADOW

Complete and Unabridged

LINFORD
Leicester

First published in the
United States of America

First Linford Edition
published March 1994

British Library CIP Data

Corby, Jane
  Nurse of Greenmeadow.—Large print ed.—
Linford romance library
I. Title II. Series
823.914 [F]

ISBN 0-7089-7519-4

Published by
F. A. Thorpe (Publishing) Ltd.
Anstey, Leicestershire

Set by Words & Graphics Ltd.
Anstey, Leicestershire
Printed and bound in Great Britain by
T. J. Press (Padstow) Ltd., Padstow, Cornwall

This book is printed on acid-free paper

For the real-life Judy . . .

1

"**I**S this seat taken?"

Judy Jordan looked up into the bluest eyes she had ever seen and thought, at the same time, he was the homeliest young man in the world. None of his features matched. His mouth was wide and thin-lipped, yet his chin was not merely cleft; it was dimpled! His eyebrows were brown and bushy, but his hair was sandy and thinning at the temples. His jaw was square, as if he were determined; his nose was thin and aquiline, as if he were too aristocratic to fight.

"No, it isn't," she said, and with an audible sigh picked up the magazines she had brought to read. This young man probably would not leave her time to read; he looked like the talkative type. But then, in the brief span of her twenty-two years, Judy Jordan had discovered most men were the talkative type when they were with her.

This young man deposited his hat and newspaper on the seat to claim ownership, and walked down the aisle looking for a place to put his large bag on the luggage rack. He came back after a minute and slumped in the seat beside her, frowning.

"Why they don't make these luggage racks big enough . . . " he said disgustedly, and opened his newspaper to the stock market quotations. He did not look at her again, and Judy flipped her magazine pages with some surprise. This young man was not running true to form.

She could appreciate his feeling of frustration; she had felt the same way herself a scant ten minutes before. She had thought, because she was traveling in the middle of the week — on a Wednesday — at the very end of August, when most vacationers were returning from Massachusetts to Grand Central, the train leaving New York would be uncrowded. There should have been no problem about seats, therefore, or even about leaving luggage on the floor.

Instead, Judy Jordan had found herself waiting in a crush of would-be passengers, all of them carrying not only two suitcases, as she was, but some also laden with packages of various sizes and shapes, with bags of golf clubs and fishing tackle and even with cartons, awkwardly tied. She had been pleased to find a seat alone; she might have known it was too good to last.

The train stopped briefly at One Hundred and Twenty-fifth Street and then slid on past the new uptown projects in the Spuyten Duyvil area and on towards Connecticut. Judy sighed again. Perhaps the trip was a mistake after all; perhaps she should have stayed on at the Park View Hospital instead of taking a job with an arthritic old woman who had already hired — and fired — five nurses.

"Come now; it can't be that bad!"

"You don't know anything about it," Judy said before she thought. The last thing in the world she wanted to do was to engage in conversation with this homely young man on a three-hour train journey. On the other hand, since he was a stranger, it might be a relief to talk out her problem with someone who could view it from an impersonal angle and then walk out of her life forever.

The young man folded up his newspaper and slipped it neatly down beside him in the seat. "Sometimes it helps to talk about a shattered romance," he said with a smile. Judy suddenly discovered that while his features did not change, they became unimportant when he smiled. He merely looked kind and intelligently interested.

"I didn't say anything about a romance."

"You didn't have to. Anyone with satin hair as bright as the color of a chestnut and golden eyes, not to mention — " he peered at her closely

— "the trace of a dimple near the left hand-corner of her mouth — anyone who looks like that is bound to be concerned with a romance, shattered or otherwise. It's elementary, my dear Watson."

"You seem to be quite a psychologist," Judy commented, unable to keep the dimple from appearing. "However, if I'm going to tell you the story of my life, I think we should at least introduce ourselves."

"I'm Jock Campbell, off on what you might call a long weekend to visit an old college chum of mine. I live and work in New York — Wall Street."

"Jock?"

"With a name like Campbell — what do you expect?"

"It figures. Well, I'm Judy Jordan, also of New York and most recently attached to the staff of the Park View Hospital. I am a registered nurse."

"I won't make any of the obvious cracks about you being too pretty to

5

work," the young man said considerately, "but I am consumed with curiosity. You must think a great deal of this young man — whoever he is — to get all teary-eyed when you even think of leaving New York. Why don't you just say 'yes'?"

Jock Campbell had put his finger so unerringly on the focal point of the problem, Judy began to talk to him as if she were arguing with herself.

There was nothing the matter with Peter Bayliss, she explained to the attentive young man beside her. He was a lawyer, attached to the office of a judge, and undoubtedly would have a fine career. He was handsome and only two years older than herself, and she had known him ever since she had been in nurses' training.

Not even parental opposition had been offered when Peter proposed, Judy said sadly. In fact, her mother thought Peter was quite wonderful, and her father enjoyed talking with him and discussing the court cases which were featured in the news. She herself also liked him so much that she had been afraid to stay in New York and date him regularly for fear she would say yes to his proposal without really being in love with him.

"You're running away!"

"I am not!"

"But you are, no matter what you call it. You didn't say yes; you wouldn't say no; you left town."

"I am not running away," Judy repeated. The phrase, she added bitterly, had been used before about her decisions. When she had determined to take up nurses' training, for instance, instead of teaching, her father had accused her of running away from the academic traditions of the family.

"Father is a professor of English," Judy added, "and no Jordan was ever a nurse. The only doctor is on Mother's side — he's a second cousin."

But Jock Campbell did not smile. He said he had not used the phrase 'running away' in the usual sense.

To him it meant getting out of a rut or going off a familiar road to explore unknown highways. This type of running away should be encouraged, he thought, because there were so many people who simply accepted the channel into which their lives had flowed. Therefore they never realized their potential; they accepted the first set of circumstances they encountered.

"I'm about to try to solve a case which illustrates my point for a friend of mine," Jock continued. "My friend's grandmother was born and brought up in a comparatively small New England town. Her husband was moderately successful. They built a comfortable — even ornate — home. Her son, now dead, was even more successful than his father, and her grandson has, in my opinion, a brilliant career ahead of him in the business which his father founded."

"You're making out a wonderful case for the person who does *not* run away," Judy observed. "The grandmother has

8

had a fine life, a splendid home and all material comforts. What more could anyone ask?"

His friend, the grandson, should ask for more, Jock Campbell said earnestly. His grandfather's money had long since been exhausted, and he himself was supporting his grandmother's white elephant of an estate, simply because he did not want to hurt the old lady by telling her she was trying to preserve a way of life that was no longer practical.

"I'm a little confused," Judy said. "I can understand why your friend's grandmother wants to keep the home where she was so happy; but why should it be such a burden to maintain the place?"

It was a burden, Jock Campbell said grimly, because the house had thirty rooms, was set in a park-like area of twenty acres and required a staff of five to maintain it. There was even a summerhouse — a gazebo — which was not only useless, but boarded up!

More than that, from the end of August until the middle of May, the grandmother insisted upon having an 'at home' every Friday night, to which her large circle of friends and all their families unto the third generation were invited.

"It seems to me," said Judy, "Your friend's grandmother is likely to resent any attempt on your part to interfere. I rather expect she will throw you out of the house when you suggest she mend her high-living ways. If she hasn't listened to her grandson, it would seem she couldn't care less what *you* think about her and her *fin de siècle* setup."

"Whit — short for Whitney — and I are planning a surreptitious approach to the problem," explained Jock. "We're going to change the old lady's point of view, instead of forcing our opinions on her. We're hoping to make her *want* to sell the house."

Judy looked skeptical. "What's your strategy?" she demanded.

First of all, said Jock, they were going to sell her the idea that she would acquire considerable money by disposing of some of her antiques to the highest bidder.

"A respectable way of adding to one's budget," agreed Judy.

"After this foot-in-the-door approach," Jock went on, "Whit feels maybe, once the old lady finds herself in possession of some cash money, she may enjoy the sensation. She has seen very little cash since her son died, because Whit handles all the estate finances. Perhaps, come Christmas, she will consider selling the house itself and the twenty acres which keep a salaried gardener jumping — only a step ahead of the crabgrass."

"Your friend Whit has his work cut out for him, and he may succeed, since he *is* her grandson. But where do you come in? Won't you seem like an interloper?"

"It happens my hobby is tracking down antique furniture," said Jock, and

Judy, eying him in surprise, noticed he flushed beneath his heavy tan. "This enormous old house is full of rare pieces."

"Wall Street and antique furniture seem as far apart as the poles," Judy remarked dubiously. For a second she thought about telling him of her mother, who was vastly interested in antiques. In fact, her mother was by way of being an expert; she had traveled far and wide gathering material for a series of 'amateur collecting' books which were well known. It was on the tip of her tongue to ask Jock if he was familiar with any of her mother's books, but she quickly repressed the impulse. Instead she asked politely if he had seen any of the grandmother's treasures.

"Oh, yes!" Jock Campbell evidently felt on safer ground. "I've spent lots of weekends with Whit in the old house. The furnishings are impressive."

"Really?" drawled Judy. "Early American, old English, or just lost, strayed or stolen French pieces from the Palace of Versailles?"

Jock glanced at her suspiciously. "There's an interesting dining room set," he said, "which we thought I might offer to buy first. It's in a sort of yellowish wood."

"Probably golden oak," murmured Judy.

"Probably," agreed Jock. "I didn't really examine it, you understand. The chairs have high backs and are carved — gobs of carving. You can't lean back without getting jabbed in the neck or the small of your back."

"Well, one doesn't usually loll at the dinner table," said Judy hopefully.

Jock laughed, to show he shared her sense of humor. "But the seats are cushioned in tapestry," he added seriously, "and are comfortable enough."

"Gobelin, perhaps," mused Judy, thinking the brash young man would certainly understand her reference to the priceless tapestries of centuries before. But he said only:

"Huh? Oh, I wouldn't know."

Jock Campbell was lying in his teeth, Judy reflected grimly. Why? What he didn't know about antiques — tapestry or furniture — would fill several books in her mother's series. Then why was he pretending? The poor old lady, Judy thought compassionately. Something ominous was afoot between the grandson and this supposed friend of his.

There must be a plot to get hold of the old lady's possessions. Perhaps Whit was not in on it; he might simply be a decoy. This Wall Street antiquarian might be concocting a scheme which would even do away with the grandmother! She wondered if the old lady had made a will and in whose favor it might be.

Frightened by her own thoughts, Judy changed the subject. If this Jock Campbell was concerned with some nefarious scheme, it would be best to act as if she suspected nothing, at least until she was safely away from him.

"How far are you going?" she asked

casually. "I'm getting off at Springfield, myself. I expect a car to meet me there and to drive a few miles farther north."

"Springfield is where I get off, too," said Jock. "I'm headed for a little village called Greenmeadow."

"Oh!" Judy was silent a minute, staring out of the window. "What's your friend's name — his full name?" she asked. "Do you mind telling me?"

"Arthur Whitney Beyer," answered Jock promptly. "Why do you ask? Aren't we ships that pass in the night? You're not frightfully interested in his problem, are you? He's a man you never heard of before and whom you'll never meet in the ordinary course of events."

How wrong he was, Judy was thinking, but she said only:

"I felt like putting a name to your friend, that's all, since I now know so much about his difficulties. I'm always interested in people," she added.

"His grandmother is Mrs. Melissa

15

Whitney Beyer," Jock went on, apparently relieved to get off the subject of antiques.

"And she's entirely dependent on her grandson's bounty?" Judy asked. "Sounds like a TV movie."

"She may have money of her own salted away," Jock said. "But Whit doesn't think so, and he hasn't been able to find any proof of it. Anyway, he's been providing for her in the manner to which she became accustomed as a young bride. And she insists upon living this way without regard for Whit's bank account. Of course it's a big bank account, and so he's humored the old lady in the past.

"Now, however, his fiancée — a very beautiful girl, by the way; I've seen pictures of her — objects to having him throw good money after bad. The place is a liability. Elaine has put her foot down: Whit must cut his grandmother's allowance and use his fortune intelligently, as she calls it. She's already picked out a fine cooperative apartment in New York, and she wants to buy a modern winter home in Florida. Whit told me he once suggested they cut expenses by living with his grandmother after they were married, but I understand Elaine had hysterics."

"I don't blame you for trying to help your friend out of his dilemma. Trying to please two women of opposite views — one of them his bride-to-be — must be excruciating. When money is involved, everything becomes even more difficult."

"I hope we can get Whit's grandmother to listen to reason in time," said Jock. "Money from the sale of the house and grounds and furniture could bring in a tidy income, if invested properly."

"And since you're in Wall Street, you could suggest a good investment broker . . . "

"Of course, as an investment broker, I'd like to get the business," Jock said sharply. "Where's the harm in that? Most of my clients know I'm reliable."

"And you so young!" marveled Judy in mock admiration.

"The world today belongs to the young," Jock said severely.

Judy did not answer. She was thinking of her new assignment, which she had accepted because it took her out of New York. Doctor Ephraim Everett, chief of staff at the Park View Hospital, had recommended her for the post. She was to be nurse-companion to a difficult, elderly woman who was a long-time friend as well as a patient of his. The woman had had a stroke two years before, but had recovered the use of her faculties. The only reminder of her misfortune was the loss of the use of one leg.

"Her illness did not improve her disposition," Doctor Everett had told Judy. "She's always been difficult, but now she's almost impossible. I've sent her five different nurses in the past year, and she made life so miserable for them they would have quit, if she hadn't fired them first. But somehow I think you're the girl who can handle her, Judy, tantrums and all. And since you told me you would like to get away from New York . . . "

"Well, here we are in Springfield!" announced Jock. "Show me your luggage and I'll take it down for you. A car will meet you? Where are you bound for — eventually?"

"Greenmeadow," said Judy, smiling demurely. "I'm going to Mrs. Melissa Whitney Beyer's home, The Turrets. The long black car at the station must be the one she sent for me."

An elderly chauffeur had come forward and inquired respectfully if she was Miss Jordan as she stepped from the train.

"That's right!" said Judy. She looked at Jock, who had opened his mouth and forgotten to close it.

"And I'm to pick you up, too, sir," said the chauffeur. "How are you, Mr. Campbell?"

"Fine, Devlin, just fine," Jock said absently. "You witch!" he whispered as they moved toward the car. "You beautiful two-timing witch! Why didn't you tell me before I gave away all my secrets?"

Judy looked at him sideways out of dancing golden eyes. "You were telling me so many of your 'secrets' I couldn't get a word in edgewise," she said.

2

IT was an unexpectedly long drive from the Springfield railroad station to Greenmeadow. The Beyer house, The Turrets, was shortly beyond the village; in fact, the village had grown up on land which had once belonged to the Beyer estate. Since the house was a replica of a European castle, the fortified type guarding the little village houses in medieval days, it was fitting that the village had sprung up around it.

Judy Jordan was to learn the history of The Turrets later, from its owner, Melissa Whitney Beyer. Now, as the car turned into the rhododendron-bordered drive between massive wrought-iron gates opening off the public road, she was astonished to see that the great house, which topped a slight rise, presented more turrets and gables than she had ever before observed on one building. Built of native stone with a rosy hue and with a rosy tiled roof outlined by green-weathered copper flashing, the house as a memento of another era, like the summerhouse, or gazebo, Jock had mentioned, which she could just glimpse in the distance.

"You mean Mrs. Beyer lives here all by herself?" Judy asked, turning to Jock Campbell.

"With a household staff of five — remember I told you? — including a companion-nurse, which I gather is you, for the time being. I imagine you will help plan the weekly social gatherings which draw the cream of local society through those carved oaken doors."

"But whole families with an assortment of children live in one-story ranch houses nowadays," said Judy. "This seems like such an anach — what's the word I want?"

"Anachronism," said Jock. "That's exactly what it is. You see how right Whit is to try to persuade his grandmother to sell. Someone might remodel it as a nursing home or perhaps as a special school . . . "

"But I don't blame Mrs. Beyer for wanting to keep it as it is," said Judy dreamily. "I think it's beautiful. And if Whit has enough money to keep it up . . . "

The car swerved around the drive and came to a stop in front of the double oak doors Jock had mentioned. Just then one of the doors was flung open by a tall young man whose pale hair caught the sunlight as he advanced, grinning, across the flagged open porch.

"Hi, Jock, you big baboon! Glad you could make it. And this is . . . ?"

"Judy Jordan, nurse, who is running away from romance," Jock told him, chuckling. "This is Whitney Beyer, Miss Jordan."

"You treacherous beast," Judy hissed, "that was privileged information! How do you do, Mr. Beyer," she said formally.

"Call me Whit," the pale young man invited, and Judy murmured:

"Judy to you, then."

"Welcome to The Turrets," Whitney Beyer went on, shaking hands. "Granny will see you upstairs."

He led the way into a great hall which intensified the impression of a medieval castle. The floor was flagstoned with huge colorful woolen rugs scattered about, one leopard skin rug before the immense fireplace and a stag's head above the mantel. On either side wide archways opened into huge, ornately furnished rooms with heavy carved chairs and tables; the windows were obscured with floor-length starched lace curtains and damask draperies. It was a house built for entertaining — in a bygone era.

A red-haired girl whose prettiness was marred by a discontented expression appeared suddenly in one of the archways.

"Elaine, darling, come and meet our guests," said Whit. "This is

24

Judy Jordan, Granny's new nurse-companion."

"Another one?" drawled the redhead. "Every time I come into this house I meet a new nurse."

Whit ignored the comment. "And this is Jock Campbell — you've heard me speak of old Jock-o."

The sullen stare with which Elaine had acknowledged Whit's introduction of Judy Jordan changed to a brilliant smile as the red-haired girl turned to Jock.

"You spoke of him, darling, but you never told me about his big, beautiful blue eyes . . . "

"Knock it off, Doll," said Jock, seizing her outstretched hand and drawing her close so that her topknot of bright hair brushed his shoulder. "I could get personal, too, if one Whit Beyer were not around . . . "

"In that case, come with me," laughed Elaine. "We'll go out to the patio where we can be alone while Whit briefs Granny's new nurse. The old girl has been raising ructions all day; I know my poor badgered sweetheart is anxious to have someone — if she is competent, that is — take over."

Whit turned to Judy as the pair withdrew, apparently not at all disturbed by Elaine's warm reception of his friend. Privately, Judy thought it had been a display of bad taste, and she wondered at Whit's acceptance of his fiancée's behavior.

"You may not like it here," he said, "although I don't think my grandmother is too impossible most of the time. But I must warn you — other nurses found it hard to get along with her. Granny has a talent for insulting people."

It was not the way a young man should speak of his grandmother, Judy felt, looking him over coolly. Here was a man in robust health — an athletic type who showed plainly he had enjoyed the advantages of wealth and position — judging his sick grandmother with unnecessary harshness. The woman had suffered the misery and indignity of a stroke; moreover, she was probably at least three times his age.

"The fault may not be all on your grandmother's side," Judy told him after a long moment of silence.

The pale young man's glance locked with hers. "You have something there," he admitted. "But Granny has a mind of her own, even though it's slightly off-center. She believes the world still owes her the prestige she once commanded as the society leader of the town, and she refuses to understand — or even try to understand — that she's old and the world has changed. Half the people who come here do it with tongue in cheek and only because I go along with her play-acting."

"Your grandmother's a sick woman," Judy reminded him. "That's why I'm here."

Whitney Beyer's lips tightened at her rebuke. "Perhaps to care for my grandmother is not the only reason you are here. I understood Jock to

27

say you were also running away from romance."

"My private life has nothing to do with my qualifications," Judy said hotly.

Whitney Beyer shrugged. "Anyway, my grandmother has a will of iron. She's dominated me so long I can't seem to break the pattern. But we've got to have a showdown soon. Elaine won't set the wedding date until I do something about this monstrosity of a house."

"I *like* the house," Judy said perversely. "I know it represents a way of life that doesn't exist any more, but still it has charm and dignity . . ."

"And costs a lot of money to run," Whit finished. "But here's Granny's lifetime maid," he added, "come to announce Granny is ready to receive you. Right, Consuela?"

"Yes, Mrs. Beyer is waiting," the maid said primly.

"Maybe after you meet Granny, you'll want to run away again — from here," Whit remarked, and Judy felt he was hoping she would do just that.

"It's up to your grandmother to decide," she retorted. "If I please her and can help her, there's no need for *you* to be concerned about me, is there?"

Judy turned abruptly and followed the maid, her back as straight as a ramrod.

★ ★ ★

Consuela belonged to Mrs. Beyer's generation, Judy thought, and must be in her sixties. But the years had not softened her outlines or her expression. She was a tall, gaunt woman whose gray hair imparted a metallic firmness to her features; to herself Judy termed her an iron woman. She led the way to an alcove at the end of the long hall where a small elevator had been installed.

"What a convenience," Judy commented. "It's something I wouldn't have expected in this house."

"It's for the use of Mrs. Beyer," rasped Consuela, "and myself, of course. No one else can use it, except when accompanying one or the other of us."

Feeling chastened and anxious to make amends, Judy smiled and inquired: "How is Mrs. Beyer feeling?"

"She's having one of her bad days," said Consuela shortly.

"Oh, I'm sorry," murmured Judy. "Do you mean she's in bed?"

"See for yourself," snapped the iron woman. "It's not for me to tell the *nurse*," she emphasized the word, "what her patient's condition is."

She held the door of the elevator open for Judy, who discovered that, instead of being in a hallway, as she had expected, she was right in Mrs. Beyer's bed-sitting room.

"All right, Consuela; you can leave us," called a loud, almost masculine voice from a shadowy corner. There was a small click as the elevator door shut behind her and the maid was wafted away to unknown floors.

The long room, arched at the end to frame a square bay window, was dazzling in the afternoon sunlight. Judy's first impression was that there was too much of everything: too much opulent, upholstered furniture; too much heavy carved wood in the tremendous bed and massive desk behind which Mrs. Beyer sat. There was too much lace at the windows and edging the doilies on the side tables and cabinets and the bureau scarf; too much damask, in a deep red shade, in the coverings of the chairs, the draperies and even in panels on the walls. There were too many roses; they were thick in the pattern of the carpet and on the bedspread, and there were vases of them all around the room, so the scent was overpowering.

A deep, appreciative chuckle came from Melissa Beyer. She was a plump woman with a fresh complexion and short, tightly curled white hair; her eyes were large and light brown, almost the color of Judy's own. She was dressed in a beige satin negligee with froths of lace at the wrists and neckline.

"This room sort of gets you, doesn't it?" she asked with amusement. "Most people react that way, but you'll get used to it — if you stay. I like roses and lace; I'm the feminine type." With an abrupt change of manner, she said: "You're Judy Jordan, I suppose. I'm Melissa Beyer."

Judy advanced slowly, trying to adjust her mental picture of a wan, autocratic grandmother, desperately trying to cling to the customs of a generation long gone, to fit this sturdy, independent woman who didn't even look sick! The woman behind the desk was anything but wan; she looked vigorous, and she spoke with force and determination. She might be a difficult person to work for, but she would always be interesting!

Judy started to speak, but Melissa Beyer forestalled her.

"I saw you getting out of the car, and I also saw young Campbell with you. Did you come up from New York on the train with him?"

"Yes, I did." Judy thought it best to be noncommittal.

"Well, you've probably had an earful of my idiosyncrasies then, so I won't bore you with repeating them. I like this house; I'm going to stay here. My grandson and his friends and his fiancée — " Mrs. Beyer made it sound like a derogatory word, Judy thought with amusement — "can scheme till they're blue in the face. I like your looks," she added with another abrupt change of subject. "You remind me very much of myself at your age. How old are you, by the way?"

"I'm twenty-two," Judy said self-consciously, "and I'm sure you were very lovely. You flatter me by the comparison. But don't you want to ask about my training — or is there something you would like to have me do for you?"

"Sit down, sit down," Melissa Beyer said irritably. "I'll tell you if I want anything." She looked at Judy as she sat on the edge of an overstuffed chair. "Did Consuela say I was having one of my bad days? Never mind; you needn't answer. That woman is getting positively dreary on the subject of my health. Did Eph Everett tell you what's wrong with me?" she demanded.

"Yes. He told me about the stroke but said you'd made a miraculous recovery . . . "

Mrs. Beyer looked pleased. "Glad the old coot admitted it. Of course my right leg is all but useless; still I manage pretty well. I can even drive a car. What do you think of that?"

"I think it's fine," Judy said, "but I hope you'll let me do the driving most of the time."

Melissa Beyer did not appear to notice what Judy said. She sat, nodding her white, carefully coiffed hair as if carrying on a secret conversation with herself. Nervous under her icy stare,

Judy began to fidget.

"Keep your hands quiet," the old lady barked. "I hate people who can't sit still."

For some reason, perhaps because she had met so many different and seemingly difficult personalities in the last few hours, the remark rubbed Judy the wrong way. She stood up abruptly.

"I'm sorry if I don't please you, Mrs. Beyer," she said, keeping her voice steady, "because I do think it's important for a nurse and her patient to like and understand each other. If you find my manner irritating after you've known me only a few minutes . . . "

"If you can't stand a word of criticism — " Mrs. Beyer interrupted. Then all at once she stopped talking and drew a deep breath instead. Judy, watching her closely, felt real admiration for the way the woman had learned to mask her pain. She also knew Melissa Beyer was asking for understanding, in a way. She was

35

too proud to ask for sympathy; she did not want sympathy. So she went to the other extreme and pretended she was caustic and self-sufficient.

"I can take criticism or leave it alone," Judy said with a smile. "This time I'm going to leave it alone, because I know you're in pain. I'll help you get in bed and then massage you for a while. It will help, I promise you."

"Massage my leg!" Melissa Beyer tried to keep her voice sharp, but she didn't quite succeed. "Surely Everett told you I have no feeling in the right leg at all?"

"Surely he did," Judy said cheerfully. She went over to the bed and turned it back, then came over and stood beside her irritable employer. "So it's the *good* leg that's hurting you, and it's the one I'll massage. You must have overexerted yourself this morning, or yesterday . . ."

Melissa grunted assent as Judy helped her to her feet. She would not groan. "I can walk," she said through clenched teeth, attempting to hold onto her imperious manner. "Go into the bathroom and get the rubbing alcohol in the cabinet and anything else you want."

Judy obediently turned and went into a bathroom with mahogany wainscoting around the walls and a mahogany rim around the tub. The washbasin was sprinkled with the inevitable rose motif baked into the enamel. But she forgot the decoration as she swung open the mirrored cabinet door and saw the reflection of Melissa Beyer taking slow, painful steps toward the bed. Because the elderly woman thought she was unobserved, she allowed her features to be contorted with the pain that made her whole body shake.

It took Judy only a second to find the oil, cotton and alcohol she wanted; it took her a long time to arrange them to her satisfaction on a small enameled tray as she tried to give Mrs. Beyer a moment to compose herself.

"You have a wonderful lot of

supplies," she said cheerfully as she came back into the bedroom. She broke off sharply and was barely able to repress a shriek of fear.

Mrs. Beyer's cane had just gone cutting through the air in front of her like a projectile shot from a launching pad. It went straight and true from the bed to the gilt cabinet against the wall and struck with shattering force against the porcelain vase upon it.

Melissa Beyer, sitting on the bed, suddenly looked her age. Her face was flushed with anger, and she sobbed in a dry, tortured voice:

"My awful legs! My miserable, useless, no-good legs! You might as well pack up and leave; no nurse — or doctor either — will ever do me any good now. I wish I was dead!"

3

EVEN before she had finished training, Judy Jordan had felt — when confronted with a nursing problem — that some *alter ego* took over; she did not think of herself at all. She became another person; a nurse who could command her hands, her mind and her voice to work out the problem according to pattern. She never had to think of what to do; she acted as if someone else stood beside her and told her exactly what had to be done.

Judy knew the first problem now was Mrs. Beyer's hysteria. A nurse must not let her natural sympathy for the patient soften her ministrations. The chronic invalid should occasionally let off steam, but Judy realized it would be a mistake to encourage such exhibitions. She put down her tray and advanced toward Mrs. Beyer with determination.

"You could have hurt me with your cane, Mrs. Beyer." She put her hands against the woman's shoulders and held them firmly for a few seconds.

"Oh, I never . . . " Mrs. Beyer began, and then realized she had given herself away.

"You never do hurt anyone?" Judy asked softly. "But even so, you mustn't give way to tantrums; they're bad for you. Keep control of yourself at all times. Now lie back and I'll work on your hip — soften up those muscles."

Mrs. Beyer regard Judy with bright brown eyes in which relief was mingled with wariness. "I get so tense sometimes," she said in a defiantly apologetic voice. "I just throw the cane or anything else that's handy . . . "

"Everyone in nurses' training learns how to duck," Judy said with a grin. She could feel Mrs. Beyer relax as her fingers kneaded and stroked the muscles. "But won't you tell me what upset you particularly today?"

Melissa Beyer admitted she was facing a crisis. Elaine Peavy, her grandson's fiancée, had made no secret of her hostility toward Whit's grandmother. While her grandson was good and kind, Melissa said, she knew that he probably would take sides with his future wife when it came to a showdown.

"With a name like Peavy, I don't wonder Elaine is anxious to change it to Beyer," Judy commented.

Her patient looked up at her and suddenly gave a deep-throated chuckle. "I like you, Judy Jordan. You give me hope maybe I can beat the rap after all." The slang seemed appropriate, somehow, to Mrs. Beyer's mood. "But I'll need your help; I must have someone on my side."

The problem, seen from her employer's point of view, was quite different from the one presented by Jock Campbell, Judy found. She did not doubt it was also different from Whit Beyer's point of view, although he might be more understanding.

Melissa Beyer had maintained the big house and her way of living in spite of changing times for definite reasons, she explained. First, she liked the house, and it was the home she had come to as a bride. Second, because of her leg, she could not have an active social life in any other way than by inviting her old friends and their children to come and see her.

She realized, Melissa went on, the house was too big and so required a large staff of servants, according to modern standards. On the other hand, Consuela, the maid, Jim, the gardener, and Katy, the cook, had been with her from the time the house was built; she felt a definite obligation to keep them in their jobs for a few years more at any rate. It was enjoyable, too, to keep track of her old friends; to help them, if they were beset with problems; to watch their children grow up and develop traits which were familiar, even though the background of living had changed with generations.

"Children today are so restless," Mrs. Beyer said flatly. "No matter where they live or what they are doing, they want to move somewhere else and do something else. They seem to be eternally running away from what they know toward a field which seems greener, because it is farther away."

Judy Jordan blushed guiltily, but her employer did not notice, and she decided not to defend her generation or to interrupt Mrs. Beyer's train of thought.

"Turn on your other side," Judy commanded. As the woman rolled over, she mentioned Whitney and her voice softened.

Her grandson was a paragon, Mrs. Beyer declared, and they had understood each other perfectly until Elaine Peavy "got her hooks into him," as Melissa expressed it.

"I was really angry at Whitney only once," Mrs. Beyer declared. "When he was in college, he picked a weekend when I was away to throw a party with his friends in the old gazebo. I was particularly annoyed because Jim, the gardener, had told me the place was very shaky and would have to be reinforced. But there was no harm done, so I just boarded the place up and never mentioned it to Whitney again."

"Why don't you tear it down if it's unsafe?" asked Judy.

"I will. I only mentioned it to show how very well my grandson and I got along — before Elaine came into the picture."

Now, Mrs. Beyer went on, Whitney wanted her to sell the house and move. And as a first gesture, he had suggested selling off some of the furniture, particularly the oak dining room set. She did not mind selling the set at all, Mrs. Beyer added surprisingly, and then suddenly she yawned!

Judy felt it was almost superfluous to suggest a nap; she herself wanted to get settled in her room and think things out. As she turned to go, Melissa Beyer said urgently:

"You will help a cantankerous old woman who is fighting for her life — at least," she amended, "for her own way of life? I need someone on my side," she repeated.

"I'm on your side," Judy said instantly. "If it's no hardship for your grandson to maintain this place, I don't see why he should badger you about moving. But go to sleep now. We'll talk it over again tomorrow."

Mrs. Beyer did not hear her leave the room, Judy thought, knowing how soothing the massage had been. Consuela was in the hall as she opened the door, but now the woman looked less grim and presumably had decided her mistress was pleased with the new addition to the household.

"I'll show you to your room, Miss Jordan," she said in what was almost a gracious manner.

"I'm afraid you'll have to clean

up Mrs. Beyer's room," Judy said, following the angular woman down the long hall. "A vase on one of the side tables was broken. I hope it wasn't valuable."

"No, it wasn't," said Consuela, showing no surprise. "We buy them by the dozen; there are five left of the last order. This is your room, miss." So Mrs. Beyer, as she had suspected, made a practice of throwing her cane!

The maid held open the door, and Judy, looking at her, could not resist a smile. For all her forbidding exterior, it would be easy to get along with the maid; in her own way, Consuela was a psychologist.

The first 'at home' was to be held that very Friday, Judy learned at dinner. But she would not be expected to do more than observe and give Mrs. Beyer her suggestions afterward. This was the only reference made to the affair at dinner; anyone looking into the heavily furnished dining room, where everyone sat as erect as soldiers of the guard in order to avoid the ornate carving on the backs of the chairs, might have decided they made an ideal family party, Judy thought.

Elaine Peavy, in a misty green dress which brightened the color of her hair, was sweetly deprecating to her hostess. Whitney Beyer, as the privileged member of the company, teased his grandmother about breaking another vase, and Melissa smiled at him fondly, as if he were paying her an extravagant compliment.

Only Jock Campbell seemed ill at ease, Judy noted, and was probably worried about his pose as a judge of antique furniture. Also, there was something not quite right about his attitude toward Elaine Peavy.

If I were a man, thought Judy to herself, and I had just met a gorgeous redhead, I'd look at her with a little more interest, even if she was my friend's fiancée — unless I had known her before, but didn't want to own up to it. She was so lost in this puzzling thought she was embarrassed to find the redhead had asked her a direct question.

"I'm sorry," Judy said. "Afraid I was wool-gathering for the moment. What did you say?"

"Thinking of the man you left behind you?" Elaine asked lightly. "Well, I'll repeat: if you want to send him a souvenir — let him know that though you're gone, he's not forgotten — come down to the shop. I might have something there you'd think he'd like."

"Elaine runs an antique and gift shop," Mrs. Beyer explained.

"Not very well, I'm afraid," the redhead said ruefully. "I have no head for business, have I, darling?"

Whitney Beyer rose to the bait and assured her she had other attributes he found more appealing.

Judy could not resist saying, with a sidelong glance at Jock: "You must have many opportunities to buy antiques in this part of the country. This dining room set, for instance."

"Oh, I couldn't afford anything as handsome as this," Elaine evaded neatly.

"Anyway," Whit said firmly, "you'll have to give up the shop when we get married. I will demand all your time, darling."

"*When* we are married," Elaine repeated with only the slightest emphasis on the first word. "There are so many things to be settled, dear, before I set the date . . . "

Judy felt sure she was referring not to the disposal of her business but to the sale of The Turrets and some plan for putting Melissa Beyer high on a shelf. Evidently Whit Beyer thought so, too. He frowned at his fiancée and then shot a nervous glance at his grandmother, who apparently did not notice the remark.

Elaine Peavy's softly sentimental expression did not change. The hand lifting her cup to her lips was beautifully shaped and cared for; Judy did not know why it suddenly looked to her like the red-tipped talon of a bird of prey.

* * *

Friday night came all too soon for Judy Jordan. It was confusing, she had found, to be consulted as to the buffet supper menu, but then to hear no more about it; to be aware Mrs. Beyer was holding out for an absurdly high price for her dining room set, but not to know if Jock or Whit would meet her terms; to try to keep her employer from overexerting herself, but to be frustrated by Melissa's refusal to sit back quietly.

Anyway, most of the guests had arrived; Judy took a long breath and felt she was over the first hurdle. She went into the powder room under the hall stairs for a quick look at her make-up. One of the guests was already there — a slim, sheath-clad girl who was deftly wielding a long pencil-lipstick.

One of the teeners, Judy thought with a sigh.

It had been difficult to see how the various elements of an unintegrated 'at home' could be welded together. All ages would be represented, including the teeners — such as the girl in front of her — plus the young and unmarrieds her own and Whit's age, plus the lifelong friends of Mrs. Beyer's generation. It seemed hopeless to see they *all* enjoyed themselves. But her employer saw no problem.

"Having fun?" Judy asked cautiously.

"Not yet, but soon," the dark-haired girl responded frankly. She carefully pushed strands of hair over her forehead until they reached her eyebrows. "I'm Bimi Dowling," she added casually. "Rod Patterson is my date. Not much to look at, but a real fireball when it comes to keeping a party alive. He knew I didn't want to come to this shindig, so he cooked up something special — a real blast."

The conversation between Bimi and her date had been brief and to the point, if Judy had but known it.

"We'll have fun, all right," Rod had assured his girl as he parked the convertible as far as possible from The Turrets. "Get away easier," he explained parenthetically. "I had to show," Rod had gone on. "My grandmother's going to be here. She's an old boarding school friend of Mrs. Beyer's, and she'd cut off my allowance if I didn't put in an appearance."

"The older generation," sighed Bimi. "How degenerate can they get?"

"I think the word you mean is decrepit, not degenerate," said Rod critically. He was planning a writing career and took great pains with his own and everyone else's vocabulary. "Anyhow, my grandmother isn't decrepit, or Mrs. Beyer either. She had a stroke or something and uses a cane, but it might as well be a sceptre! Don't worry; all you have to do is speak to her; then we'll find the rest of our crowd and do the disappearing act. I've got it all set up."

"I suppose it's the same with everyone here," Bimi had said. "Families have such moldy obligations. You ought to see the way I'm tied down on Long Island, at East Hampton, where our clan spends the summers. I only got to come up here to the Berkshires because Elsa — the girl I room with at school — persuaded Mother to let me visit her. Elsa will be here tonight; her grandfather once had a thing for Mrs. Beyer, I believe. Before they each married someone else, I mean."

"That makes Elsa a member of the club, all right," Rod agreed. "Well, here we are. Did you ever see a house with so many spires and minarets?"

Bimi surveyed the Beyer mansion with awe. "Gee!" she said, and then: "Awk!"

A tall shape had disentangled itself from the overgrown rhododendron bushes in the foundation planting and stood before them, so close it

53

all but upset Rod, who had to take a step backward.

"What did you want to do that for, Clyde?" he had demanded. "Are you making like the headless Horseman or something?"

"Muffle it," whispered Clyde. "What's the layout for tonight?"

"This is for hipsters only," Rod had said in hoarse response. "Listen: you know the glen behind the house and the thing there — the gazebo?"

"Sure," said Clyde. "Mrs. B's gardener used to chase us off with a rake when we were kids."

"It's been boarded up for years, but some of the boards are loose now. Never mind how I know — I *do* know. Anyhow, it was used as kind of a playhouse when Mrs. Beyer was a bride. She used to give wild parties there — wild for her day — or that's the way I heard it."

"They must have been smashing," Clyde had said sarcastically. "Sure, I heard the old story, but I'd forgotten it. I never really believed it."

"Makes no diff," said Rod impatiently. "The place is still full of party junk: an upright piano, a set of drums, dishes, things like that. Our crowd will meet there as soon as we can drift away from the dead-end doings inside. Pass the word along."

Bimi now explained to Judy: "A bunch of us are going to the playhouse in the glen. You know, the gazebo."

Judy stood wordless, feeling a little sick. She had not overheard the conversation with Rod, but she could imagine what it had been. There had been time enough since for Bimi and the others to pay their respects to Mrs. Beyer and make a show of standing around laughing and talking, and to wait for Rod to give the signal. A few minutes ago he must have nodded, or made known in some way that it was time to adjourn to the gazebo.

"Nobody tipped you off yet?" Bimi was asking. "Well, now you know. Find your boy friend and put him wise; then follow the crowd. Better grab a few sandwiches and whatever else you can carry on the way."

Judy finally found her voice. "But the gazebo? It isn't safe!"

"Safe enough, if you don't go gabbing to the oldsters," Bimi said cheerfully evidently thinking Judy was talking about the secret plan. "Just keep it dark." She smiled gleefully and flashed out the door.

It dawned on Judy that in the gold shantung dress she was wearing and with her hair smoothly framing her face, Bimi had mistaken her for one of the crowd. Suddenly she understood the surreptitious raids on the buffet tables she had noticed earlier; the teeners had piled sandwiches and cakes on paper plates taken from a side table. But they never stopped to eat the garnered loot; they slipped through the French windows or disappeared down the hall. Judy had assumed they were going outside to eat on the terrace in the bright glow of a romantically huge moon.

But she had guessed wrong! The crowd was bound for the gazebo, and a sub-party of their own. The old structure was weak; it might collapse if too many people were in it at one time. How many were there in Bimi's crowd? More than was safe, surely.

Should she go to Mrs. Beyer right away and tell her about the secret — and dangerous-party? She would be marked as an 'informer' if she did!

No, Judy decided swiftly. She had to go herself. She had to stop this fun-fest before it got started, if she could, but at any rate before it ended — in tragedy!

4

THE way to the playhouse led through a rose garden, where the late blooms, their color washed out by the moonlight, still perfumed the air. Judy knew where the gazebo was located — in a little glen where it was out of sight of the main house. All she had to do was follow the path when she emerged from the rose garden. But what was she going to say when she reached the place?

So immersed was she in her problem that, when she caught a slight movement behind a trellis, she stood still, frightened. Then she heard a girl's low laugh — Elaine's! Relieved, she went on, scuffing her slippers on the gravel to give warning of her approach. She need not have bothered, however, she saw as she came abreast of two figures, arms entwined, heads bent together, standing in the shadow of the vine-covered trellis. Elaine and Jock! Looking resolutely straight ahead, Judy hurried past.

She had almost reached the playhouse when she heard her name called softly behind her.

"Judy!" Whit caught up with her swiftly, so purposefully she realized he must have been following her. Had he seen the two beside the rose trellis? It was just possible he had been moving so fast he had not looked in that direction.

"Where to?" Whit demanded, taking Judy's arm. "You're setting a fast pace for a girl who is just out for a stroll."

"There's a teeners' party going on in the playhouse," said Judy tersely. "I understand the place isn't safe. I've got to stop it!"

"Making like a chaperon pretty early in your stay here, aren't you?" drawled Whit. "As far as I know, the teenagers were doing all right before you arrived."

"You're deliberately misunderstanding

59

me!" flared Judy. "All I'm worried about is the safety of the building. If a dozen or so kids are dancing around, the place may collapse."

"What gives you that idea?"

"It's been boarded up, hasn't it, as unsound?" Judy's voice had an edge. Whit was implying she was just a busybody, stepping in where she was not wanted.

"Oh, boarded up!" said Whitney. "My grandmother did that to get even with me when I gave a wild party one weekend and she got mad about it. The place is perfectly safe. I'm sure of that."

By this time they were near enough to the gazebo to hear the sounds of merriment — the pounding of feet on bare boards, the tinny thumping of a long-untuned piano, the shouts and screams of laughter . . .

"Don't go spoiling the kids' fun," cautioned Whit. "If you get the teeners down on you, your life won't be worth living around here."

By the time they reached the open

door, Judy had decided her best chance of influencing the group was to pretend to be one of them. After all, Bimi Dowling had mistaken her for a teener. For that matter, not so long ago she herself *had* been on the sunny side of twenty. But had she ever belonged to a set as raucous as these boys and girls?

Everyone, it appeared, was barefoot. Most of the crowd were sitting or sprawled on the floor, while Bimi, who had taken off her dress and was draped in a big Spanish shawl which she could only have purloined from the music room in The Turrets, was doing an exotic dance. At the moment she was bending backward, bare feet planted wide apart, her pliant body curving in a graceful arc, her long hair trailing on the floor.

It was a large, square room, lit by a 'wagon-wheel' type of chandelier set with electric 'candles,' and suspended from the rafters by four heavy chains. Judy was glad to see how thick the links were, since a youth, who she learned later was Rod Patterson, was sitting on the wheel, swinging it vigorously back and forth and uttering an occasional banshee wail.

Music was being supplied by another youth, addressed as Clyde, who was banging the piano keys at rhythmic intervals with an old croquet mallet while still another, wearing blue denims and stripped to the waist, was beating time on a set of bongo drums which were showing plainly the inroads made by squirrels and field mice.

Bits of discarded sandwich, paper cups and empty soft drink bottles littered the floor, made slippery in spots by spilled soda. As Judy and Whit watched, Bimi sank down exhausted.

"Up! Up — everybody up!" shouted a teener so full-bearded Judy realized at once the beard was false. Everybody promptly leaped to his feet; a girl shoved aside the mallet-wielding pianist and, after twirling the old-fashioned piano stool, sat down and began a hot number.

Whit seized a pretty little blonde and joined the dancers, and a tall teener, with a shock of black hair and a deep dimple in one cheek, reached out a proprietary hand and yanked Judy onto the dance floor. She tried to protest she didn't know the steps, but she was caught up in the general thrashing around, the pulling this way and that, lost among the shaking hips and determined twirling in what seemed to her a senseless scrimmage. However, the others appeared to know what they were about. She realized if she kept moving in a disjointed fashion, she could at least keep clear of collisions.

It seemed to her as the dance whirled on that the floor moved slightly under her feet. Perhaps it was natural, she told herself, the way they were stomping and even, in some cases, leaping into the air and coming down heavily on the old boards. But suddenly, as they stopped for an intermission, she distinctly felt the building sway.

Whit was wrong — the gazebo wasn't

safe! Old Mrs, Beyer had been wise to board it up, warning off trespassers. But what could she do? Shout a warning to the wild crowd? Instinctively she knew she would be greeted only with jeers and catcalls. Then she had an inspiration.

"The old piano — it's out of tune!" she yelled, in one of those inexplicable hushes which often occur in the middle of a hubbub.

A chorus of "So what?" answered her outburst.

"It wants to play a hula!" shouted one of the boys. "Hey, you, can you do a hula?" he demanded of Judy.

"Sure she can!" cried Rod, dropping down from the wagon wheels as she started to shake her head. "All she needs is a grass skirt. Who's got a grass skirt?"

"Here!" Someone ripped off a piece of the matting which served as wainscoting around the walls. "Come on; give us a hula!"

The crowd surrounded her, wrapping

the piece of dusty matter around Judy's gold skirt. At the same time another youth struck up a pseudo-Hawaiian tune on the piano, and Judy, falling in to the spirit of the moment, began to dance.

She had seen enough Hawaiian-based movies to present a reasonably authentic hula, and the applause was deafening. She suddenly felt guilty. She was enjoying this and having as much fun as the others. Whit was grinning at her across the room. What must he think of her, especially when he remembered what she had told him about coming here to save the youngsters from the danger of a collapsing playhouse!

She made a sweeping bow, to indicate the end of her dance, and nearly lost her balance. How dizzy she was! No, it wasn't dizziness! The floor was definitely moving under her feet. The building was shuddering!

★ ★ ★

65

Only Whit saw the look of horror that erased the smile on Judy's face. Whit, who was crossing the room to stand beside her, raised his arm for silence.

"Listen, kids!" he shouted. "The piano *does* need a good overhauling. What say we drag it out on the lawn and give it the works?"

"Give it the smasheroo treatment!" shouted one of the boys. "Heave, ho, me hearties — heave ho!"

He ran over to the piano and began to push it toward the door. A dozen willing hands were added, and the piano was rushed out the door and onto the lawn.

"An ax, an ax, my kingdom for an ax!" howled Clyde, invading the small storeroom off the main room, where a collection of broken shovels, a rusty hatchet and other discarded tools lay in a heap. Immediately the whole crowd was streaming onto the lawn, leaving Judy and Whit to follow more slowly.

"Whew!" whispered Whit. "I wasn't sure we'd make it. Did you feel the way the floor tilted?"

"It was sickening," murmured Judy. "We'll have to figure out a way to keep them from going back in."

Outside, the boys were demolishing the piano in high glee. Under the blows of the hatchet, a couple of heavy hammers, even rocks, the piano was fast being reduced to rubble. As one after the other of the wires gave way, there came a despairing 'ping!' sounding for all the world as if the instrument were giving a cry of mortal anguish. Bits of polished wood flew about, and a group began gathering them up; soon they were blazing in a bonfire the teeners built higher and higher.

Now the wreck of the piano was complete. The bonfire crackled and sputtered, and the crowd, joining hands, danced around it, yelling like Indians. Judy and Whit stood side by side, watching silently.

When Whit finally spoke, it was to reassure Judy. "Don't feel so bad," he said. "The piano was beyond repair, and it served a good purpose in getting the kids out of the playhouse."

As he spoke, Judy laid a hand on his arm. "Listen!" she said.

Above the roar around the bonfire, they could hear an ominous crack, as if timbers were being slowly torn from their moorings. It was followed by a louder crack, like a giant fist striking the roof of the little house, and a steady crunching, grinding noise as if the building were being crushed. The war dance around the bonfire halted. Everyone stood frozen, staring at the playhouse, now shaking uncontrollably. Suddenly the roof fell in; the walls swayed outward, and crashed to the ground in a heap of shingles, plaster and beams.

Bimi Dowling was the first to speak. "We've wrecked it," she said in a small voice. The teeners looked at each other with frightened eyes.

"The building was shaky," said Whit. "Granny knew it; she had it boarded up — remember? But she should have torn it down."

"Well, we've saved her that much trouble," put in one of the crowd, trying to sound brave.

"Somebody's got to pay for the damages," retorted another boy.

"You mean us?" murmured Bimi.

"I mean probably our parents to begin with," said the boy. "And they'll probably take away our allowances . . ."

The long faces around the dying bonfire lengthened even more.

"Maybe Mrs. Beyer won't find out about it," suggested one of the crowd hopefully.

"Say!" One of the boys turned suddenly to Whit. "I know. You're Mrs. Beyer's grandson, aren't you?"

Whit nodded. "Your host," he said ironically.

"You should have stopped us!" the boy cried. "It's your fault!"

"Nothing of the sort!" said Judy

sharply. "We're all in this together. Whit shouldn't have let the party go on, it's true. But it was out of hand by the time he got here. It was too late to stop the party. We shouldn't have joined in, he and I, and we did. I started down here in the first place to put an end to the goings-on, but I didn't seem to know how."

"Who are you?" demanded Bimi Dowling. "What do you mean — you shouldn't have let the party go on? What business is it of yours?"

"Miss Jordan is my grandmother's new nurse," said Whit. "She feels responsible because she heard about your party and didn't tell Mrs. Beyer. She didn't want to be an informer, you see."

The boys and girls stared at her, abashed.

"She's a good dancer," murmured Rod Patterson at last.

"Your hula was tops," said another boy. "Professional-like."

"Thank you," said Judy, laughing,

and broke the constraint. All at once the whole crowd began to laugh uproariously, the boys pounding each other on the back and the girls doubled up, half hysterical.

"She's a good sport," said someone when speech was possible once more.

"Sure is," said another. "She's a jolly good fellow," he sang, and the others took it up.

"She's a jolly good fellow," they chorused, moving toward the big house with one accord, "which nobody can deny!"

Judy and Whit fell into step behind them.

"What are we going to tell Granny?" worried Whit. "It seems too bad to spoil her first party of the season."

Bimi Dowing and Rod Patterson had linked arms and, walking directly behind them, overheard the remark.

"We'll do what we can to make it up to Mrs. Beyer," Bimi promised. "We'll tell her what happened and take our medicine. I can't wait to see some of the parents' faces," she added. "How much does it cost to rebuild a gazebo?" she wondered.

"A lot of the cars have gone," one of the girls observed, looking along the driveway. "I hope my folks have left."

"There are still a lot here," said someone else grimly, and they all turned resolutely toward the wide screen doors.

Judy and Whit were bringing up the rear as they reached the porch. Elaine, who had been sitting in one of the porch chairs, came forward to meet them.

"Where have you been?" she demanded rudely.

"Sorry, darling," said Whit. "We were acting as a Number One Disaster Unit." He brushed by her and entered the house.

"What did Whit mean by that?" Elaine asked Judy, detaining her with a hand on her arm. "I looked everywhere for him." She was looking defiantly at

Judy as if daring her to contradict the state.

"You looked chiefly in the rose garden, I presume?" asked Judy, and took Elaine's hand from her arm.

5

MRS. MELISSA BEYER lived up to her reputation as an autocrat, a complete ruler of her corner of the world and a termagant of the first water. Judy stood to one side and watched while Bimi and Rod, who had been elected to have the dubious honor of breaking the news about the wrecked gazebo, told their hostess how effectively they had destroyed a piece of her property. Rod Patterson, since his own grandmother had gone home, injected a note of flippancy at the end of the recital.

"So that's the way the cookie — or rather the gazebo — crumbles," he said with what was intended to be a sophisticated grin. "We're very sorry, Mrs. B., and we'll work on your chain gang and put the playhouse back together again or give you a pound of flesh for every pound of worm-eaten wood we tore down. Of course I haven't got much flesh to spare," he added, looking at his lean, long legs encased in tight jersey pants. One of the girls tittered nervously.

Without moving a muscle, without raising her voice or making a gesture, Melissa Beyer proceeded to reduce Rod Patterson to the stature of an insect which would have been unwelcome in anyone's home, much less hers. She mentioned the gazebo and the parties which she had given there, and the picture she painted of a bygone era when good manners and simple pleasures were taken for granted had all the teenagers momentarily spellbound.

Then Melissa Beyer neatly brought the subject up to date by telling the youngsters exactly what they had done.

"A memory is a fragile thing" Melissa Beyer said in her deep and moving voice. "It is made up of moonbeams and cobwebs and the sound of lost laughter and the fragrance of roses which have long since withered and died. Memory is a lovely thing and when it is all you have left you learn to hold it gently and to take it out of its safe hiding place only when you are alone. For there are some people who like to destroy memories. They jeer at them and stamp on them or — like you young hoodlums — they tear down the very walls once built by love."

There was absolute silence in the drawing room where Melissa Beyer sat in a wing chair beside the fireplace. Judy Jordan felt tears pricking her own eyelids, and those of Mrs. Beyer's generation who were still there were unashamedly weeping. Bimi Dowling no longer looked like a hurt young girl; she looked like a youngster of five or six who had just been thoroughly spanked.

"If you will excuse me," Melissa Beyer said, standing abruptly and reaching for her cane, "I will go up to my room. Judy, would you please help me? I know my evening is finished, and I think perhaps my pleasure in having my friends around me on Friday evenings has been torn down, too, at least for tonight."

There was something about the last remark which did not ring quite true to Judy, and she knew, as her employer leaned heavily against her arm going down the hall toward the elevator, Melissa was limping far more than she ordinarily did.

But she made no comment and, even as she helped Mrs. Beyer undress and, at her request, gave her a soothing back rub, was careful not to say anything or even to meet Mrs. Beyer's eye. Melissa was comfortably ensconced in bed with her carafe of water, a small volume of poetry and her reading glasses beside her on the bedside table before she spoke.

"Think I was too rough on them?"

"No," Judy said slowly, "if it is truly the way you feel about it. But I couldn't help remembering the gazebo has been boarded up for many years.

You yourself said it was a hazard and should be torn down. Also, some of those youngsters could have been badly hurt; the loss of your precious memories should be compensated for in part by thankfulness that no one was maimed for life."

Melissa Beyer sighed. "I might have known you'd see through me. Of course I don't care about the miserable old eyesore. But, after all, my grandson Whitney and Elaine want me to sell the dining room set. I've got them over a barrel because of the thoughtless actions of these youngsters, and I'm darned well going to take advantage of it."

Judy kept her face straight but was aware she had little control of the dimple at the corner of her mouth. "How much are you asking for the oak dining room set Jock Campbell came here to buy? I don't want to pry, but I gather you rejected the first offer."

"Certainly I rejected it," Melissa Beyer

said, thumping her pillow vigorously. "They offered me five hundred dollars. Five hundred dollars! Ridiculous!"

"It may be worth more to you," Judy said cautiously, "but actually, Mrs. Beyer, a golden oak dining room set has a very limited market, and therefore a reduced valuation."

"I don't care about the valuation," Melissa Beyer said grimly; "what I care about is the money. I have something special in mind, and I will need two thousand dollars to carry it through. If Elaine Peavy has my grandson so wrapped around her little finger that he will force me to sell my furniture, then I'm going to make it just as difficult for her as I possibly can. Whitney will now give me the two thousand dollars I ask to soothe my feelings about the ruined gazebo. But Elaine Peavy is going to be as mad as a wet hen when she hears about it. I'll make her sorry she ever tried to cross Whitney's poor old decrepit grandmother!"

With a smile of pure malicious glee,

her employer wished Judy good night and picked up her book of sentimental poems.

* * *

Melissa Beyer never did mention the oak dining room set to Judy again. Judy could not help smiling cynically to herself as she remembered her employer's gushingly sentimental references to the ruined playhouse and her fond memories of it. Apparently Mrs. Beyer was the type who could cherish her memories or forget them, just as the whim suited her.

It was late Sunday afternoon and Mrs. Beyer was resting in her room when Judy came downstairs. She had considered going for a walk, mainly to work off the effects of Katy's very excellent Sunday dinner, but the ground was still wet; in fact, soggy in spots. So, deciding against going out of doors, she went to the library, intent upon finding something she might keep in her room and read from time to time when she had a free minute.

There was a single light burning in the big room lined with bookshelves, and Jock Campbell was seated in a leather easy chair, scowling at the oriental rug.

"Oh!" Judy said, taken by surprise, "I thought you'd gone back to New York. I'm sorry," she apologized instantly. "I didn't mean to sound so ungracious."

"It's all right," growled Jock. As Judy had noticed before, when he was not smiling he looked very homely indeed. "Believe me, the next time I come here I'll bring my car. Phooey on waiting around for Whit to say farewell to his lady love."

"My, we're in a foul mood," Judy commented. "But isn't it pretty nice of Whitney to drive you all the way back to New York? I mean, if he has to turn around and drive right back up here to Greenmeadow . . ."

Whitney would not be driving back the same night, Jock explained, still sounding rather surly. He maintained a small apartment in New York, and while he usually stayed at The Turrets and commuted to the factory in northern Connecticut, he could also go there directly from his New York place.

"I know his father started the factory," Judy said idly, looking over a handsomely bound set of Dickens' works, "but Mrs. Beyer never mentioned what it is they make."

"It's got something to do with electronics."

"I don't know anything about electronics."

"Even if you did know, Whit wouldn't tell you what he makes. It's very hush-hush." Jock got to his feet abruptly and walked over to where she stood in front of the bookcase. "For heaven's sake, take pity on me and come out and talk to me in the patio. You must know Dickens by heart."

"Almost," Judy admitted. "He's one of my favorite authors. But that isn't the reason I'd like to talk to you for a while."

Jock Campbell brightened visibly, put his hand under her chin and tilted her face until she was looking directly into his extraordinarily blue eyes.

"The Campbell charm," Jock said with a grin. "It never fails to work. But for a while there I thought you were the exception that proved the rule."

"Hot mon!" Judy adroitly side-stepped Jock's reaching hands and moved behind a leather-topped table. "I will admit your charm, bold sir, but at the moment I was seeking information from you."

Jock Campbell, with a pretense of heartbreak, said he would give her whatever information she was looking for. He followed Judy back to the main hall and then to the wide glass doors which opened into what everyone called the patio.

It was in reality more like the paved

courtyard of a castle, although on a small scale and backed on only two sides by the masonry of the house. A watery sun was breaking through the clouds, and Jock turned over the wicker chairs and set them upright. In the sheltered corner they were quite comfortable and could even recapture for a moment the warmth of the fading summer.

Now that she was in a position to ask Jock about the sale of the dining room set, Judy realized she was putting herself in the role of an inquisitor. But Jock saved her the trouble.

Melissa Beyer had finally signed a bill of sale for the oak dining room set, he explained, but had held out for the impossibly high price of two thousand dollars. He had a blank check with him, Jock added, but of course that was only by arrangement with one of Whitney's friends. Whit himself was buying the set and would remove it and put it in storage. Judy congratulated him on accomplishing the mission he had come from New York to carry out.

"It isn't a matter of congratulation," Jock said sourly. "Whit's grandmother pulled a fast one. I don't mind admitting to you now that I really don't know a darned thing about furniture, but I do know the dining room set isn't worth two thousand dollars; I doubt if it's worth two hundred."

"Anyway," Judy said soothingly, "now that Mrs. Beyer has sold some of her furniture, it may be easier for her to be persuaded to sell more — eventually to sell the house. Have you talked with her yet about investing the money she now has?"

He had talked with Whit's grandmother, Jock said gloomily, and had gotten nowhere fast. Melissa Beyer claimed that the loss of the dining room set had put her in such an emotional state she could not discuss just yet what she would do with the money. And she could not imagine going into the dining room and looking around at the place where her beloved pieces used to stand. He would have to come back another weekend. Then she would discuss what she was going to do with the two thousand dollars.

"Perhaps I can help you a little," Judy said dreamily. "I am sure if Mrs. Beyer puts another dining room set in place of the oak one, she will never be happy in the room. I'm going to suggest she make a few changes in the morning room — which is big enough for a dining room anyway — and equally close to the kitchen. Then the dining room can be changed into a game room. If I am going to be responsible for the programs of the Friday at homes, I think we ought to have something more to offer the teenager. A ping-pong table perhaps, or a game of darts . . . "

"You're a doll," Jock said with enthusiasm. "I'm sure Whit will go along with your idea. When I get Mrs. Beyer's investment account, you must let me wine and dine you as a token of my appreciation."

"Are you asking me for a date?" Judy said directly.

"Sure I am," Jock retorted. "Don't tell me you're still carrying a torch for that guy in New York. And anyway, can't I ask you out to dinner without having to pledge eternal devotion?"

"You make me sound quite naïve," Judy said angrily. "But that isn't what I meant. On Friday night, as I was going down to the glen, along the path that runs through the rose garden . . . "

"You saw me kissing Elaine," Jock Campbell said, his eyes crinkling with amusement. "So you think I'm a dastardly cur and unfaithful to my friend Whitney and all that sort of thing. Well, maybe you're right. But I knew Elaine long before she met Whit; in fact, I'm quite fond of her. However, Elaine is a girl who sees herself as a bride, and I'm not quite ready to settle down."

"Is there any particular reason you and Elaine concealed the fact that you knew each other from Whit?" Judy demanded.

"Well . . . " Jock did look embarrassed now. "When Whit and I were in college together, I said some things about the girls I was running around with at the time, and I wouldn't want him to get the idea I had been referring to Elaine when I told him any one of these escapades. But why are we talking about Elaine Peavy? I want to talk about you. You're far more beautiful than she is, Judy Jordan."

"That isn't true," Judy said vehemently. "Elaine Peavy is strikingly beautiful. Her gorgeous red-gold hair and her complexion and even the way she walks — as if she were a goddess or something — are out of this world."

"This isn't the time or place for me to tell you about yourself," Jock said, getting slowly out of his chair. "Whit's car just turned into the drive, and it's my guess he'll want to get started on the trip back. Anyway, I want a nice, quiet romantic corner and a great big moon — the harvest moon will do — soft music and all the background touches a girl should have when a guy is making love."

Jock pulled her to her feet, and his blue eyes looked into hers so deeply that in spite of herself Judy thrilled to their admiration. She laughed a little shakily.

"At least you've given me fair warning," she said.

"Not a warning; a promise." Again Jock's fingers tilted her chin so that she had to look up at him, and this time he bent his head and kissed her lightly on the lips. "Until we meet again," he murmured, and vanished into the house.

6

THE morning sun was pouring gold into the kitchen windows when Judy came down for her breakfast. Katy the cook was short-handed these days. Her young assistant, Euphemia, who had been married the year before, was now at home expecting her first baby. To save Katy extra steps, Judy had insisted on taking her breakfast in the kitchen.

"I love this kitchen; it's such a happy-looking room," said Judy. "And you, Katy, are such a happy-looking person yourself. It's fun to eat breakfast here."

Judy had heard lurid tales of the reception accorded nurses by run-of-the-mill household help in many homes, and she was agreeably surprised when Katy, instead of grumbling and muttering imprecations under her breath, seemed genuinely glad when Judy had at first timidly suggested that she'd eat in the kitchen mornings.

Now she carried the coffeepot over from the stove and poured herself a steaming cup on a side table near one of the sun-flooded windows.

"Mrs. Beyer feels like having an egg this morning," she remarked, as Katy brought her buttered toast and set a glass of orange juice before her. "I think poached."

"What's the matter with a fried egg?" demanded Katy. "Mis' Beyer had a fried egg yesterday, and I didn't hear any complaints."

"Nobody is making any complaints," said Judy. "But in view of Mrs. Beyer's condition, I think a poached egg would suit her better. I know it's a little more trouble; in fact, a really fine poached egg is something many cooks can't manage. But you're such an expert — I'm sure you can turn out a real first-class poached egg."

Katy, who had been about to explode

into protests and point out that she had only one pair of hands˙ and there were the day's meals to plan, plus any snacks that might be called for, relaxed under this praise and began assembling the utensils necessary for an egg masterpiece.

"Poor Mis' Beyer is lucky to get a nurse like you, Miss Jordan," she remarked, complimentary in her turn. "The flighty creatures she's had to put up with — you wouldn't believe. The last one was on a diet — couldn't eat this, couldn't eat that. She was reducing, she said, on doctor's orders. I had to take more trouble with her meals than Mis' Beyer's."

"Well, if her doctor insisted . . . " began Judy placatingly.

"Humph!" grunted Katy. "She was out to make work for me, that's all. I don't believe in this reducing business anyway. I think that if you're fat, you're fat, and if you're thin, you're thin, and monkeying with Nature is my idea of flying in the face of Providence."

"But some people have to reduce for their health's sake," Judy murmured.

"That's just superstition," Katy sniffed. "There was Hattie McCombs. She weighed two hundred and forty, and when she broke her toe and had to go to a doctor, he said she'd have to take off some weight."

"Sounds reasonable," said Judy, pouring herself a second cup of coffee.

"Funny way to treat a broken toe, if you ask me," said Katy.

"Well, I don't suppose he was treating the broken toe, exactly, by having the woman reduce; just taking some of the extra weight off, so that it would heal more quickly, and at the same time improving her general condition. Of course he did what was necessary for the toe, too," Judy observed.

"I think I'll make a lemon meringue pie for dinner," said Katy thoughtfully. "Speaking of Hattie McCombs reminded me of it. She liked any kind of pie. Cake, too."

Judy supped her coffee and looked around the kitchen. It was the largest kitchen she had ever seen, apparently designed for the preparation of huge dinners and party meals. Along one wall was an enormous range; along another were three refrigerators and a freezer.

"You have a lot of storage space for food," remarked Judy.

"Oh, there's only one refrigerator and the freezer in use," said Katy. "The others are old-fashioned ice-boxes, put in when the house was built. Mis' Beyer would never hear of them being took out. She likes to hang onto old things, you know."

"I noticed you said Hattie McCombs liked pie and cake. Do you mean she stopped eating them because the doctor told her to?"

"I should say not!" Katy began to squeeze lemons in the electric squeezer. "Hattie never put any stock in doctors' new-fangled notions. She went on making and eating pie and cake — you should have seen her seven-layer chocolate fudge cake with walnut icing — till the day she died."

"Oh," said Judy, "she died then."

"Eating whatever she wanted right up to the end," said Katy cheerfully. "What do you want I should send up with Mis' Beyer's egg — two or three pieces of toast?"

"I think one piece of whole wheat toast will be enough," said Judy. "If you get it ready now, I'll take it up to her. You will be busy getting breakfast for Mr. Whitney, I suppose."

"Never," said Katy. "Mr. Whit never eats breakfast here. He leaves about seven-thirty and drives to the works in Connecticut. Says he don't need nothing till the morning coffee break. Now my husband always said the way to start the day was with a good breakfast — ham and eggs or steak and fried potatoes and a good hunk of pie. I always had three or four pies on hand, so he could take his choice."

"I don't think I want any breakfast after all," said Melissa Beyer peevishly, when Judy settled the breakfast tray across her knees as she sat up in bed. "I especially don't like the looks of that egg."

"Katy took a lot of pains with it," Judy coaxed. "It's a poached egg."

"I don't want any breakfast," repeated Melissa. "But if I did, I'd want grilled lambs' kidneys and hot muffins. I was reading a book where these people — English they were — had grilled kidneys in a warming dish on the sideboard and they all helped themselves. It sounded very appetizing."

"We'll have to try it some day," Judy said soothingly. "Now don't let your egg get cold."

"I don't like the way it looks at me," retorted Mrs. Beyer. "It's a one-eyed egg."

Judy, annoyed as she was, decided to laugh merrily. "That's awfully funny," she said, unfolding a napkin and laying it across Mrs. Beyer's lap. "Here's looking at you!" She broke the egg yolk and spread a spoonful of egg on a bit of toast, bringing it up to Melissa's lips. The eldery woman opened her mouth, accepted the tidbit and chewed it with enjoyment.

"That's just the way I like eggs," she said. "Here, let me fix a bigger piece of toast. Do you know what day this is?" She reached for her glass of orange juice and ate the toast and drank the juice alternately.

"Why," began Judy, "it's . . . "

"Friday again!" interrupted Mrs Beyer joyously. "My at home day."

"How could I have forgotten that?" murmured Judy, who hadn't.

"I don't believe," Mrs. Beyer went on, eating her egg with apparent enjoyment, "we have to do anything special about the menu this Friday. I think Consuela and Katy between them can handle that. But I do need your advice on something else."

"The dining room looks awfully bare," Judy said, anticipating what her employer's problem was. "As a matter of fact, I was wondering where we were going to eat tonight."

"What do you think of using the so-called morning room?" Melissa Beyer asked. Judy could see she was enjoying this opportunity once again to assert her authority in the house by changing the routine. "There's a drop-leaf table over against the wall which is large enough for the five of us."

"Jock and Elaine Peavy will be here?"

"Jock Campbell had better be here," Melissa Beyer said grimly. "And he'd better bring the two thousand dollar check. Of course Elaine will always be among those present. She says she doesn't approve of my at homes, but I notice she hasn't missed one in the last two years."

Judy had deftly removed the tray to a side table and brought the massage tray from the bathroom. Mrs. Beyer had been delighted with Judy's massaging and declared it helped her and kept her from getting so very tired.

"What did you want to ask my advice about?" Judy inquired.

"The empty dining room, of course," her employer said, burying her face in the pillow. "There's no problem tonight, I suppose. Whitney said he would borrow a hi-fi set from one of his friends, and any of the youngsters who want to dance can go in there. But what will we do from here on in? The dining room can be seen from the front hall, and it would give me the willies to see it so bare every time I looked inside, as if I had already moved out and didn't know it."

Judy was sure that Whit and Jock had urged Mrs. Beyer to sell the dining room set for that very reason — to make her feel that she was already leaving the place. But looking at the generous proportions of the wood-paneled room, Judy had been struck by a thought and she proceeded now to mention it to her

99

employer, as she had to Jock.

The room was ideal for a playroom, she pointed out. At one end there could be a billiard table; a darts game might be set up between the windows, and card tables could be stacked in the built-in cabinet against the wall. There were so many games to interest people of all ages nowadays, Judy added, that it was likely the Friday at homes could become well-known in Greenmeadow and invitations would be sought by every one.

"You're a bright girl, Judy Jordan," Melissa Beyer said happily. "And you think the same way I do. I know just where I can get that billiard table. Heindrich Shoen has one in very good condition. You must have seen the man last Friday. He's a big white-haired German fellow, one of my old beaus, as a matter of fact. His granddaughter Elsa was here. I believe she goes to school with Bimi Dowling. Well, no matter. Next week you can help me get the equipment we'll need to turn the old dining room into a game room."

"Perhaps I shouldn't mention it," Judy said hesitantly, "but how will your grandson like the idea of using the money you get from the dining room set to buy equipment for a game room? I got the impression that he and Jock Campbell expected you to invest the two thousand dollars."

Melissa Beyer snorted. "I can't help what Whitney and his friend think I'm going to do," she said, sitting up with a militant air. "I will not be dictated to in my own house. I have made plans for spending that two thousand dollars, and it doesn't include investing even a penny of it. I think that's enough of the massage, Judy. Send Consuela in to help me get dressed, and then I won't need you again until about five o'clock."

"You are very generous in giving me time off, Mrs. Beyer," Judy told her employer, "and I will try to make myself useful with preparations for tonight. But I do think there must be something more I could do for you personally."

"Yes, there is," Melissa Beyer said, and her brown eyes held an unexpected twinkle. "Whitney said he'd be home early, but I don't want to be bothered seeing him at lunch. So I'm going to ask him to take you to a colonial inn about thirty miles from here. They have excellent food, and in back of the restaurant there's a country store where you can look around even if you don't want to buy anything."

"But maybe your grandson doesn't want to take me to lunch," Judy said in alarm. "He may have planned to go somewhere with Elaine . . . "

"No, she has to stay in her shop," Melissa Beyer said shortly. "This luncheon date is an order, Judy, and it won't be just a social occasion. I want you to take full responsibility for turning the dining room into a game room. You're to tell Whit that it's entirely your idea. He'll have lots of objections and I don't want to be bothered listening to him. My mind is made up."

"So, you're hiding behind my uniform," Judy said severely. "And speaking of uniforms, don't you think it would be better if I wore one during the day?"

"Can't abide them," Melissa Beyer retorted. "In uniform, you keep reminding me that I am almost an invalid. Anyway, I like color. That yellow linen suit is very becoming."

"Thank you," Judy murmured. "You realize, of course, Whit is going to give me a hard time. He has every right to resent my interference in the household."

"It's your problem" Melissa Beyer said serenely. "My suggestion would be to make my grandson fall in love with you."

Judy discounted what her employer had said, of course, but she became increasingly nervous as the hours went on. The job was not exactly as Doctor Everett had described it to her. She had expected to find a woman who had been crippled by a stroke, and who was more or less resigned to a passive role in her daily life. She had been prepared to ease Melissa Beyer's physical distress and to help her keep up her social contacts as much as was possible for a shut-in.

But her employer would never be a shut-in, Judy thought grimly, even if she were flat on her back or in a wheel chair. She was a born autocrat, a household dictator who would brook no interference with her plans. If she, as a trained nurse, were to stay in the household, she must make up her mind either to take sides with Melissa Beyer or to help her grandson and his fiancée force her employer into a quieter and more retired life.

When she had reached this point in her reasoning, Judy knew she had made her decision. Melissa Beyer was making a gallant fight, and her grandson Whitney had many years ahead that he could enjoy in that house or anywhere in the world. It would not hurt him to give up a short time to humor his grandmother's whims. And if at the moment she wanted a playroom, she, Judy Jordan, would consider it as much a part of her care for the semi-invalid to give her a game room as to give her a daily massage.

7

PERHAPS because she was in a belligerent mood, Judy was critical of Whitney Beyer's attitude when he invited her to the Hearthstone Inn in Leicester. The village was only thirty-five miles away, but to Judy's sensitive ears Whit was making it sound like a trip to the moon. His expression, too, was so carefully noncommittal that if she had been a free agent Judy would have refused the invitation on the spot. This pale young man, with the sunlight gleaming on his blond hair and emphasizing the fit of his striped blazer over his square shoulders, had no reason to treat her like a bond servant!

Judy retaliated by saying nothing at all as they drove along back roads to the Hearthstone Inn. The dark blue convertible was a beautiful car, and

Whitney handled it with effortless ease. The day was sparkling and clear, and the leaves were still green, although a faint scent of wood smoke signaled the coming of autumn. Everywhere along the road the gardens were a riot of color, and near a greenhouse they passed a whole field of dahlias whose heavy heads nodded in the slight breeze. It was a perfect day for driving through the countryside with a charming and eligible young man, but Judy, remembering Mrs. Beyer's suggestion that she encourage Whitney to be romantic, had to smile ruefully. If the young man beside her tried to embrace her, Judy thought to herself, she would instinctively duck. He did not appear to be in a romantic mood.

"Granny has a bee in her bonnet, to use an old-fashioned phrase," Whitney Beyer said at length. "I suppose eventually you'll break down and tell me what this is all about. But what I can't see is — why the elaborate buildup? Why couldn't we have had lunch at the house as usual? I generally come home on Fridays and go down early to the village to pick up Elaine."

"I'm sorry to interfere with your plans," Judy said stiffly, "but you must remember your grandmother is my employer and I follow her instructions. Believe me, if I weren't obliged to do it, I wouldn't accept your kind invitation to drive all the way to the Hearthstone Inn for a boiled New England dinner or whatever we're going to have."

Whit Beyer glanced at her quickly, and his expression softened. "I agree with you I have not made this date seem attractive," he said quietly. "But you must understand my position. I'm trying to plan constructively for the future, and my grandmother's attempt to divert me by having me take you out to lunch doesn't fool me for a minute. I know she doesn't like Elaine, and she's trying to break our engagement. I'm about fed up with her machinations."

"You make this luncheon date sound

like a Summit Conference." Judy said impatiently. "Believe me I repeat, I have no intention of disrupting your plans for the day. But as your grandmother's nurse, I feel we should let her run the house in her own way, especially since they're rearranging the morning room so we can eat there instead of in the dining room."

Whitney parked the convertible in front of a pleasant white brick building with a huge bay window looking out over the river that bordered one end of the place. If she had had a more agreeable companion, Judy was thinking as they walked across the flagstone terrace, the luncheon date might have been a very pleasant one indeed. Someone like Jock Campbell, for instance, she told herself, and blushed at the recollection of how charmingly gallant the homely young man had been.

There were many adjectives which could be applied to Whitney Beyer, Judy decided during the next hour, but charmingly gallant he was not. Even the waitress, dressed in an appropriate colonial costume and a voluminous starched apron, realized this was no lovers' rendezvous. Whit growled out their order and then sat moodily staring out the window, as if he wished the meal were already over.

"What about this man you were engaged to in New York?" he asked suddenly, fixing his pale gray eyes on her as if she were a strange specimen, Judy thought resentfully. "Why are you running away from him?"

"If we are going to discuss my love life," Judy said sharply, "let's get the facts straight. First, I was not engaged to Peter Baylis. Second, I am not running away. I took a job at The Turrets because Doctor Ephraim Everett, the chief of staff at Park View Hospital, thought I could help your grandmother adjust to a new mode of life. He was not at all concerned with my private life; he was thinking of me as a registered nurse. I would suggest you think of me that way, too — as a nurse-companion to your grandmother. Perhaps then you could treat me more as a person and less as a constant source of irritation."

For some reason this seemed to amuse Whitney Beyer. He explained again at some length how concerned he was with his grandmother's future and how much he wanted her to sell the house and either go to a nursing home or live in a small apartment which could be maintained at a reasonable cost.

"You still haven't answered my question about Peter Baylis," he reminded her in a milder tone. "Why don't you invite him up here? I am sure Granny would be glad to include him in her invitations to an at home."

"Your grandmother has already mentioned inviting Peter up here," Judy told him, looking with interest at the oyster cocktail the waitress had just set before her. In spite of her resolution to react sparingly, she felt she could let down the barriers just a bit and enjoy at least this first course. Whitney Beyer seemed to approve of her decision.

"The oysters are good here," he said, spearing one of them. "I'm fond of oysters, but I don't often get to eat them. Elaine is allergic to sea food."

Judy tried to look properly sympathetic, but she was not too concerned over Elaine's dietary problems. She changed the subject to describe the time she had gone to visit some commercial oyster beds in Long Island Sound. Whitney Beyer apparently enjoyed her account of the trip, and Judy was congratulating herself on having smoothed over a difficult situation when her luncheon companion exploded another bombshell.

"We seem to have covered the home life of the oyster pretty thoroughly," he commented with what Judy thought was a hateful smile. "Now, if you don't mind, I'd like to talk about my home life for a while. Exactly what is my grandmother planning that requires such an elaborate approach on your part?"

"Sorry if I've been boring you," Judy snapped. "I made a suggestion to your grandmother this morning which she liked and which she wanted me to talk over with you. However, if you would prefer to discuss it at another time — when you are in a slightly better mood — I'll be only too happy to wait awhile."

"I am all ears."

"You make it very difficult."

"You said you had a suggestion. Let's hear it."

"Even if it's good you won't like it."

"Probably not."

"Okay then, like it or not. I think you ought to change the dining room into a game room. The younger people who come to your grandmother's at homes need something more than a plate of food and conversation. That's especially true of Bimi Dowling and her crowd. The room does look awfully

113

empty since the dining room set set was taken away."

"All right," Whitney Beyer said. "You've made your suggestion and I don't like it. In fact, I won't have it. The whole idea of persuading Granny to sell the dining room set was to leave that room empty and give her cash which she could have fun with in the stock market. I am not going to let you throw a monkey wrench into my plans. The room stays empty."

"It was just an idea," Judy murmured, "and it was your grandmother's idea that I should be the one to speak with you about it. Beyond that there is nothing more to say. But I'd be willing to make one little bet with you before we close the subject."

"Bet?" Whit asked suspiciously. "What do you mean?"

"I'd be willing to bet," Judy said slowly, and she made no effort to keep her eyes from dancing, "that your grandmother has not waited to hear your reaction. I'll give you odds we'll find the dining room already has a billiard table and hi-fi set installed by the time we get home."

* * *

Judy would have collected her bet, but she did not see Whit alone again during the entire weekend. It was odd, she reflected as she dressed on Monday morning, how two people living under the same roof could still manage to see each other only at a distance. It was because the house was so big, Judy supposed, as she buttoned her blouse and picked up her cardigan. Or it could be that Whit had been careful to avoid her.

He seemed to have recovered his good humor after a brief session with his grandmother before the at home started. Melissa Beyer had proved herself a person of surprises. Whitney had accused her, she told Judy on Sunday, of deciding on a game room to keep the teenagers occupied during the at home sessions. But, Melissa reported with a chuckle, she had told him a fact about his old grandmother that he had not known. She had been an expert at billiards in her youth, and gambling at bridge was one of her few vices.

Of course when he heard that, Judy reflected as she went down to breakfast, Whitney had been entirely agreeable to having the dining room made over into a game room, at least for the time being. But Elaine Peavy had not been so happy about the arrangement. She had found Judy alone for a few minutes on Friday night and she had said, without preamble and with no attempt to disguise her animosity:

"Whit tells me it was your bright idea to turn the dining room into a game room. I don't know what your plan is, Nurse Jordan, but you are interfering with *my* plans, and I won't have it. We have been trying — my fiancé and I — to get Mrs. Beyer to sell off her furniture room by room and eventually to sell the house."

"But I didn't mean . . . "

"I don't care what you mean," Elaine Peavy spat at her. "Just concentrate on your nursing. If you get any more bright ideas about what Mrs. Beyer should do with the rooms in this house, keep them to yourself. That's a warning."

Judy could only stare as the redhead turned and marched away, apparently satisfied that her ultimatum would be obeyed. Judy wondered briefly what Elaine would have said if she had known about the game room discussion with Mrs. Beyer. But there was no point in discussing anything with Elaine. She was clearly a declared enemy in the household, as far as Judy was concerned.

Katy was not in a talkative mood when Judy reached the kitchen. She did not seem upset, but she was clearly preoccupied as she served breakfast and prepared another meal. Judy thought of asking her why she was baking a ham and fixing all the trimmings so early in the day, but she decided against it. She took up the tray that Mrs. Beyer had ordered the night before and found her employer not only awake but sitting up and going through some papers at the desk.

"I'll skip the massage this morning, Judy," she said with a great show of efficiency. "We have a great deal to do today. Just put the tray over there near the bed. How is Katy coming on with the cooking?"

"Fine," Judy said more puzzled than ever. "I can't figure out why she is preparing a full course meal so early in the morning."

"Because I told her to," Melissa Beyer said. She left the desk and came over to where Judy had set the tray. "We are going to take that ham and the vegetables and some salad and dessert over to poor Euphemia. She's the kitchen maid," she explained, as Judy looked blank.

"I heard she was sick," Judy commented.

Poor little Euphemia was rather a pet of hers, Mrs. Beyer explained, spreading her toast liberally with marmalade. She came from a large family and had come to work at The Turrets two years before. She had liked the job and had gotten on so well that, when her family moved away, she had stayed on in Greenmeadow and Katy had given her a room.

"Then Pheemy met this young boy who really is more or less a harvest hand. She fell in love with him, and they were married some months ago. Now she's going to have a baby, and her husband, Dick Ferris, has gone to work over in New York State, on a turkey farm."

"Where is Pheemy living?" asked Judy.

"That's another problem," Melissa Beyer said ruefully. "Dick bought this run-down place about fifty miles from here, and they were not going to live in it until next summer. But in the meantime he lost his job nearby and could get work only with this New York State farmer, and Pheemy got sick, and so everything is sort of in a mess. I'm worried about the child not having enough to eat, and I know she must be terribly lonely. So we're going to drive over there this morning, you and I, and bring her some food and see what else she needs."

"Do you do this — I mean, play Lady Bountiful — to all your hired help?" Judy asked.

"No, of course not!" Melissa Beyer said vehemently. But there were telltale spots of color in either cheek. "In the first place, the kitchen girls and the girls who help Consuela come and go. They are usually self-sufficient. But poor little Pheemy needs help, and I feel bound to do what I can."

Judy stood looking at the plump, white-haired woman sitting in the luxurious if old-fashioned bedroom and thought to herself that no matter what the modern world thought of her generation and the way it had spent money on elaborate homes and expensive trappings, there was still something to be said for the type of person who would pause to take care of an unfortunate servant who had no claim on her.

"Do you think I'm being foolish?" her employer demanded, as Judy still did not speak. "I'm afraid Whitney would not approve of what I am doing. He would want me to get in touch with a welfare agency, I suppose. But I'm sure they have a lot of people to take care of — and I don't like to think of poor little Pheemy asking charity from strangers."

"Yes, I think you're being foolish," Judy said, but she could not help smiling. "It's a grand kind of foolishness, and I am proud and happy to be part of it. How soon can we get started?"

8

"THIS must be the place," said Melissa Beyer, slowing the car and peering dubiously at a two-story house — weather-beaten, apparently on the verge of collapse. A long veranda ran across the front of it, but its roof had sagged to a point where it slanted toward the ground at one side. The steps had disappeared; the front door had no knob.

"It looks abandoned," said Judy.

"No, it's the right place. I used to visit here many years ago, when it belonged to a family I knew well. It's a late eighteenth century house, once a showplace, with hand-hewn beams and hand-wrought door hinges. But that was — I hate to think how many years ago . . . There's Pheemy, coming out the side door."

Still apprehensive over the condition

of the house, Judy helped Mrs. Beyer from the car and, when the older woman had descended, reached in for the basket of food they had carefully packed.

"Judy, this is Pheemy," said Mrs. Beyer. "Judy Jordan, Pheemy, has been looking after me because, as you know, Whit doesn't trust me to behave myself."

"Oh, Mrs. Beyer! How good of you to come to see me! I'm so lonesome here since Dick went to work in New York State. He gets home weekends, but . . ."

The girl's eyes filled with tears which she tried to blink away. Judy, carrying the basket on one arm, put the other around Pheemy's thin shoulders. "We understand," she said soothingly.

"To think you'd come all the way to see me," gulped Pheemy. "I'm not really crying," she said to Judy; "I'm just awfully glad to see Mrs. Beyer again."

It was a brave attempt to control her

123

feelings, and Judy squeezed the girl's shoulders as they went into the kitchen. It was in an appalling state of disrepair. Melissa Beyer, however, calling on all her social aplomb, looked around with a warm smile.

"A wood stove!" she exclaimed. "My grandmother used to say there was nothing baked bread like the oven of a wood stove."

But Pheemy wasn't deceived. "I can just imagine what Katy would say if she could see me."

"Katy misses you," said Mrs. Beyer tactfully. "She has refused to let me hire anyone to take your place. Says any of the girls I suggest to her would be more trouble than help around *her* kitchen."

Judy had begun taking the food out of the basket. "The ham is still hot," she said, setting it on the table. "Katy's compliments."

Pheemy watched as the various items appeared, including a seven-layer chocolate cake which Katy had insisted on making. "Pheemy loved all my cakes, but she was wild about this layer cake. It's my own recipe," she had said proudly.

"Now you just sit down and eat," said Judy, seeing the longing in the girl's eyes. "Pheemy, I want to see you polish off this plate . . ."

"But aren't you going to eat, too?" Pheemy asked, looking at Mrs. Beyer.

"It's sweet of you to ask us," said Melissa, "but we can only stay long enough to have a cup of coffee. I've got a business engagement."

Judy knew Mrs. Beyer had no such engagement; she also knew that her employer meant to leave all the food for Pheemy. "Fine thing, if we sat down and ate up Pheemy's food!" she told Judy later in the car.

Now, however, as she drank the coffee which Judy made on the old-fashioned stove, Melissa chattered about the old days and the family who had lived in the ancient house. She told about the five children who had kept the place in an uproar, and coaxed an understanding smile to Pheemy's pale face.

"I'd like to look around the old rooms," said Mrs. Beyer, after a while, and Judy guessed that she was leaving the nurse alone with Pheemy, so she could question her about her health.

"You must be careful about things like chopping wood," Judy said gently.

"Oh, I don't chop any wood. Dick leaves me enough for the week when he goes away," said Pheemy eagerly. Then she looked at Judy, hesitating and coloring before she spoke.

"You're a nurse, aren't you? A real nurse?" she asked.

"I'm real enough," laughed Judy. "I don't look as if I'd fade into thin air at any minute, do I?"

"I just mean . . . " Pheemy laughed, too, then stopped suddenly. "I wanted to talk to somebody who knows about what happens when a girl is having a baby. Miss Jordan, I'm so scared!"

"I think that's because you don't

understand what is happening," said Judy slowly. "You are having a wonderful time — I mean that literally — and you ought to be able to enjoy it. I have some books which I want you to read. They tell you in simple language what to expect, so you will not be surprised and frightened at the changes you undergo from time to time. How old are you, Pheemy?"

"I'll be eighteen this month."

"What a lovely age to have a baby! You're so young you and your child can grow up together. I suppose you have a name already picked out?"

"If it's a boy, we're going to call him Richard — after Dick, you know. If it's a girl, Dick and I want to call it Melissa, after Mrs. Beyer."

Judy noticed Pheemy was brightening as they talked in this casual way about the baby. All the girl needed was reassurance, she thought, and told Pheemy she would come to see her whenever she could.

"Also, there's a very fine doctor in

a New York hospital where I worked," she told the girl when she and Mrs. Beyer were leaving. "His name is Doctor Everett, and I'll ask him to stop in to see you next week when he's in this part of the country to address a medical group."

"Oh, we couldn't afford to pay a New York doctor," said Pheemy, turning scarlet. "Dick wants me to have the best, but . . . "

"There won't be anything to pay. He can send his bill to me," interrupted Melissa Beyer.

"That won't be necessary either," said Judy. "I have a standing offer from Doctor Everett to act as a free consultant in any case I suggest while I'm away from the hospital. It puts me under obligation to return to the hospital when I can do so, he says."

Even Pheemy was laughing as Melissa and Judy left.

* * *

"Not everybody has a social conscience as active as yours, Mrs Beyer," said Judy as they drove home.

"Social conscience!" snorted Melissa Beyer, "I suppose that's a new-fangled word for trying to run other people's lives."

"Not exactly." Judy stared appreciatively out of the car window at the brilliant autumn foliage along the side of the road. "It's trying to help other people run their own lives. There are many movements going on today with that kind of goal — adult education projects, housing improvements, hospital development. They provide an outlet for people with social conscience, who realize they can't do a great deal individually to help others, but that as a group they may accomplish important results."

"I suppose you know what you're talking about," said Melissa. "I don't. People who try to help in a small way, as I'm trying to help Pheemy, would, it seems to me, accomplish as much, when you add their achievements all together, as a lot of people all working together for the same thing."

"That's not quite the way it turns out," said Judy. "It takes a lot of time and effort and money to help just one person, but when the same time and energy and money is welded, so to speak, it goes further. Ten people individually helping ten different people can help many more than ten if they pool their efforts."

"I happen to like helping Pheemy," said Melissa. "It's a personal matter between us, and that's the way I like it. I don't want to have to sit around listening to committees talking about helping people I don't know and don't want to know. Talk, talk, talk — I couldn't stand it."

"But a lot of people sit around and talk at your at homes," Judy reminded her. "You enjoy that. You'd probably enjoy even more talking with a group who wanted to do something constructive."

"Nonsense!" exploded Melissa, as she turned the car expertly to avoid an oncoming truck. "Wants the whole road, I guess," she added glaring balefully into the rear-view mirror at the truck she had just passed.

"Anyhow, I'm too old to start joining up with a lot of cranks with harebrained ideas," she concluded.

Melissa Beyer seemed to be resisting her suggestions with all her might, Judy was thinking as they neared home, but the chances were she would think it over and realize in time that Judy was right. She understood Melissa's way of reasoning very well.

She knew, for instance, that while Melissa might admit to herself that a marble fountain she now wanted to install in her garden served no useful purpose beyond fostering her own satisfaction in owning something she had always longed to possess, she would defend the purchase not as a way of satisfying her own whim, but as a means of providing work for the plumbers or pipe fitters or whoever would be called upon to install it. She would refuse to admit that setting up an outmoded ornament of this type in a garden behind a house — that had also outlived its reason for existing as a private home — was a waste of time and money which might have been employed more usefully in helping to provide better housing in city slum areas.

However, desperately as Melissa Beyer might try to cling to her own point of view, her native shrewdness and honesty as well as her innate desire to help others might very well bring her to the realization of the truth of what Judy had been saying.

Melissa Beyer can't be forced to change her mind about selling her house, which, although I sympathize with her and enjoy the place as a charming reminder of other days and ways, is the only sensible course. But she can be led to do just that because it will give her the opportunity to embark on a new way of life, Judy told herself. She doesn't know it now, but she really wants to catch up with modern living.

* * *

They reached The Turrets to find Peter Baylis waiting for them.

"Peter!" Judy ran into his outstretched arms as if she were indeed the fiancée she had been designated by Whitney.

"Judy! I couldn't wait any longer for an invitation to visit your hideout." Peter grinned at her crookedly in the way which had always made Judy's heart skip a beat.

"Why didn't you let me know you were coming? And it's not a hideout; it's the place where I work. Have you been waiting long? Mrs. Melissa Beyer, this is Peter; you've heard me speak of him."

"In the warmest words," said Melissa.

"I can imagine," Peter observed wryly. "Now, answering your kind queries, Judy, I didn't let you know

133

I was coming because I didn't know myself until I was on my way. I had an urgent call from a client more or less in the neighborhood and decided to drop in on you, for which I hope Mrs. Beyer does not blame me. And I haven't been waiting long but would have waited as long as required, because I wanted to see you, Judy."

Judy had never realized that Peter's eyes were not only gray, but steely. He fixed his gaze on her now.

Just like an attorney for the defense, cross-examining a reluctant hostile witness, Judy thought, and managed to suppress a giggle.

"It's nice to see you, Peter," she said quickly, forcing herself to be serious. Peter seldom found anything to be funny, she remembered, and felt he would not appreciate any levity at the moment. She hoped the dimple at the corner of her mouth was not showing; it had a way of contradicting her most dignified air.

"I hope you can persuade Peter

— may I call you Peter? — to stay a few days," put in Melissa Beyer.

"I'm flattered at having you call me Peter on this very brief acquaintance," Peter told Melissa. "And I'm sorry I can only stay a few hours. I've got to return to New York tonight."

"Well, at least we'll see you at dinner," Melissa returned. "Meanwhile, Judy, suppose you show your visitor around the place."

"I'd love to," said Judy. "Sit down a moment, won't you, Peter, while I take Mrs. Beyer up to her room?"

"Nonsense, child, I can manage the elevator by myself."

But Judy took Melissa's arm and rode the elevator with her. "I'll send Consuela up with a cup of tea and some cinnamon toast. We skipped lunch, remember."

"Oh, be off with you!" retorted Melissa Beyer. "That poor young man has already been waiting all afternoon for you."

"He said he hadn't been waiting

long," Judy said perversely, but she shrugged and went downstairs.

"Perhaps you'd like to see the view from the east corner turret," she began briskly as Peter rose to meet her. "You can see for miles over the countryside, and with the foliage so colorful . . . "

"Can we be alone in the turret?" demanded Peter. "Or is there any likelihood of being trailed there by gnomes or elves or any of the troop of fey folk who are undoubtedly responsible for keeping this spellbound edifice in order? Surely they can't have enough ordinary servants to run this labyrinth of furniture-cluttered rooms!"

"Oh, Peter, it's quite a lovely house! I'm enjoying it here," said Judy.

"Waiting on a whimsical old woman hand and foot," remarked Peter.

By this time they had reached the second floor corridor and were walking east to a small door that opened on the very end of the hallway. When Judy opened the door, they were confronted by a narrow winding stairs which led to a little tower room.

"There! Isn't that a magnificent view?" asked Judy, gesturing toward one of the slit-like windows through which could be seen a series of hills, marching off as far as the eye could see, each bedecked with bright red and gold-topped trees, interspersed with clusters of dark evergreens.

Peter glanced out of the window and turned back to Judy.

"Magnificent," he pronounced. "Now that we've seen the view, let's get down to the basic reason for my visit — our marriage."

"Why, Peter . . . darling . . . "

"Judy, beloved, I never hoped to hear you call me darling in just that tone; not the way a girl says 'darling' to just any acquaintance, but the kind of 'darling' that means, 'Yes, I'll marry you.'" He put a finger under her chin, tilted it up gently and bent to kiss her on the lips.

"Let's make the wedding very soon," he murmured.

"But," Judy protested, "I haven't said . . . I don't know . . . "

"But you love me!"

"I don't know," said Judy. "Give me a little time, Peter."

"Time!" cried Peter, "Time for what? To see if someone else will make you a better offer? Has all this wealth and extravagance gone to your head? Oh, Judy, don't stall me off again!"

"Please, Peter." Judy was close to tears. She really liked Peter. Why did he have to be so arbitrary? "I've been so busy here, I haven't had time to think . . . "

"All right, Judy; I'll let you go on wasting time at the beck and call of a selfish old woman . . . "

"She's not!" cried Judy. "She's been most considerate."

"Considerate!" Peter threw the word right back at her. "I'm talking of *love*, my dear girl, and you talk of an employer's consideration. If you want to weigh one against the other, by all means do so, if you're determined to waste your time. But I'm not wasting my own time — not any more of it. Let me know when you want to see me again — but make it soon, very soon, Judy!"

He turned and hurried down the turret stairs, with Judy following as closely as she could. Downstairs in the main hall, he turned to her.

"Goodbye, Judy," he said, touching her cheek lightly with one finger.

"But aren't you staying to dinner?"

"I couldn't eat a mouthful," said Peter grimly. "Please convey my thanks to Mrs. Beyer. Explain that I've remembered an early evening appointment."

9

PETER BAYLIS had given her
an ultimatum. Perhaps that was
not the proper way to think of a
proposal, Judy told herself many times
in the next few days, but it was the way
she felt about it, nonetheless. If she was
going to waste her time catering to a
rich woman's whims, even though she
was a semi-invalid and liked to have a
trained nurse with her, Judy was giving
him the runaround, Peter had implied.
Perhaps she was!

Yet actually there was more to the
situation at The Turrets than met
the eye. Actually, her employer was
at the turning point in her life; her
whole future would be decided in the
next few months. Would she gradually
sell off the furniture, one room at a
time, and then, pocketing the money,
redecorate? Already the dining room

had been turned into a game room, and the morning room had become a really charming dining room. What could Mrs. Beyer do with the library, if she sold all the books? And how about the living room, the butler's pantry, the kitchen itself?

At this point in her attempt to discover what her employer had in mind, Judy usually gave up. It was, in fact, hard to keep her mind on anything indoors as the trees turned the countryside into a careless riot of color, changing from day to day and effectively distracting the mind from any serious, mundane thoughts. It was a lovely mellow, languid season, and it invited enjoyment and avoidance of any change.

Even Whitney Beyer was affected by the picturesque procession of the days. Nowadays he often returned to The Turrets early and had dinner with his grandmother and Judy. He frequently teased her about her billiard tournaments with Heindrich Shoen; his manner toward Judy was relaxed and friendly.

Judy had expected the at homes would be curtailed or skipped for a while when the youngsters went back to school and college, but although there were not as many as on the first night, Melissa's creation of a game room drew the younger crowd back from the colleges not far away, and the older group played bridge with enthusiasm or developed billiard tournaments of their own.

Even Elaine Peavy seemed to have lost some of her resentment of Melissa Beyer's calm assumption that everything would continue in the future as it had in the past. Elaine was skillful at billiards, Judy discovered, and enthusiastic about the game. It was surprising at first. Judy discovered Elaine's delight in making trick shots; in leaning backwards over the table so that her beautiful figure showed to advantage; in calling her shots in a clear, triumphant voice that made every masculine head turn to watch her play. Elaine Peavy, Judy thought, was a difficult adversary, even for Melissa Beyer. The billiard table Whit's grandmother had installed so defiantly was now a showcase for the beautiful redhead!

So the at homes continued with no apparent change in the routine and no lack of interest on the part of those invited. Judy, consulting with Consuela and with Katy on the refreshments to be served each Friday night, made sure there was enough for at least thirty guests, and it was seldom there was anything left over which the resourceful Katy could not use the following day.

Yet every once in a while Judy had a twinge of uneasiness about the smoothness of life at The Turrets. The better she came to know Melissa Beyer, the more stubborn and set in her ways she found her employer to be. And as she came to know Whit Beyer a little better, too, she could not help but admit he was right. The way of life his grandmother was trying to perpetuate, while pleasant, belonged to another era and another generation. Whitney Beyer could not change himself or his point of view, either. It was a deadlock, yet both Whit and his grandmother were ignoring their differences for the moment. It was the lull before the storm.

But, uneasy as she was, Judy had no premonition, one bright October day, that the storm was about to break. Whitney had left work even earlier than usual and joined his grandmother and Judy at lunch. Melissa was delighted to see him, and Judy wondered, as his eyes sought hers, why her heart should thump so loudly. It must be obvious to anyone as keen as her employer, Judy thought, that there was an electric current which had entered the room with her grandson and touched off a spark Judy was powerless to control.

"In case you ladies are wondering why I played hooky," Whit said, accepting the plate the little maid hastily set before him, "I will not keep you long in doubt. Granny, I want to kidnap your nurse for the afternoon."

"Aren't you feeling well?" Melissa inquired in an elaborately innocent manner.

"I feel wonderful, it's a wonderful day, you are looking wonderful, Granny dear, and I think it would be perfectly wonderful if you would let Miss Judy Jordan escape into the countryside for a look at the beautiful foliage. The frost is on the punkin and the corn is in shock — or words to that effect."

"A miserably inadequate quotation," Judy said coldly, but she could not keep her eyes from dancing. "Your grandmother and I already have plans for the afternoon. We are driving over to check on Pheemy and perhaps pick up some baskets of apples and squash and a pumpkin or two. All the farms are advertising their surpluses."

"Judy, dear," Melissa said hastily, "I'm not quite up to all that riding today; I decided before lunch. There's no reason Whit shouldn't stop by Pheemy's . . . "

"No reason at all," her grandson said cheerfully.

"And you can get the apples or squash, or let them go until another time. I do this mainly to please Katy; she likes to have a well-stocked cellar at the beginning of the winter. There's no reason at all you shouldn't drive around with Whit."

"I suppose not," Judy said doubtfully, and Whit looked pained.

"Could you put a wee bit more enthusiasm into your acceptance?" he asked. "I'm not an ogre, you know."

Judy laughed at him and flew upstairs to get the baby clothes she and Melissa Beyer had had such fun buying. For some reason she could not fathom, she felt this was a special holiday — a mood which persisted during the drive to see the expectant mother, whom she described to Whit as they rode along.

"Is Granny helping our former maid, Euphemia — what a name! — in a financial way?" Whit asked just before they arrived at the ramshackle farm.

"Oh, no!" Judy said. "I don't believe your grandmother thinks of generosity in terms of money; she has a generosity of the heart — a real concern for Pheemy's welfare. Anyway, I'm sure Pheemy and her husband wouldn't accept charity; they are fiercely independent."

Their visit to the Ferris farm was unexpectedly brief; Pheemy, looking particularly well, invited them in but explained that a neighbor was helping her to put up pickles. Judy brought the packages into the aromatic kitchen, greeted the motherly-looking woman at the stove and relayed Melissa's good wishes. She was back in the car again in less than five minutes.

The holiday mood persisted as Judy directed Whit to farms which were selling their produce in bushel baskets and barrels. Since she was not too familiar with the countryside, her directions often took them onto back roads or on the wrong roads, and at one time they were definitely lost.

"You are one girl I like to be lost with," Whit told her with a smile.

"Being lost is definitely better than being shipwrecked," Judy said philosophically. "I think if we turn right down here, we'll get back to the main highway."

"Shipwrecked?" Whit asked in surprise.

"Yes." Judy found herself blushing. "Don't you remember when you were in school, you'd sometimes get into long discussions about being shipwrecked and who you'd want with you on a desert island? When you said what you did about being lost . . . "

"I see what you mean," Whit said gravely. "And I think if you decide to get shipwrecked, instead of lost, I'd like to be along then, too. Please let me know so I can arrange it."

"We have a date," said Judy with equal gravity. And then they laughed together so gaily a squirrel paused on his way up a pine tree and looked at them in surprise.

Whit insisted, when they were on their way back to The Turrets, that he treat her to the 'harvest special' at a shining lunchroom near the highway. It was a concoction featuring a double scoop of ice cream, covered with butterscotch sauce, fruit cocktail, whipped cream and nuts, and Judy, who had protested she wanted only a soft drink, was ashamed of herself for attacking it so heartily

She was chewing the last maraschino cherry when Whit said suddenly.

"Would you have any idea what my grandmother intends to do with twenty-five hundred dollars?"

"Twenty-five hundred dollars?" Judy repeated stupidly.

"I gather she didn't mention such a sum to you."

"She certainly didn't! Is she going to buy something?"

Whit shook his head. "I don't know. But Ben Horton is the head of the bank where I maintain a checking account for Granny, and he lets me know if the account gets low. He told me this morning Granny called him and asked if she could write a check for twenty-five hundred without having it bounce. He told her it was all right — and it is — but it will leave her with only a few hundred in the account. Ben thought I ought to know."

"It *is* a large amount," Judy agreed. "Why don't you ask her what she's going to do with it?"

Whit shook his head. "It wouldn't be quite cricket, as our British friends say. Granny has two thousand dollars from the sale of the dining room set; she evidently intends to add five hundred to it, and maybe she will invest it all."

"Through Jock Campbell?"

"Jock hasn't said anything to me," Whit said slowly, "although it's possible Granny wants to make it a surprise."

Privately, Judy doubted that her employer intended to invest any part of the money, but she thought it wise not to say so. Anyway, it was getting late, and she was anxious to get back to The Turrets. She shivered as she settled herself in the car, and Whit asked with a smile:

"Someone walking over your grave?"

"No," Judy said, "but I feel apprehensive. Probably I'm just being silly and, as you said, she is going to invest the money in something, whether she's thinking of using Jock Campbell's services or not."

"Before we get back to our problems," Whit said, his eyes on the road, "I want you to know this has been a wonderful afternoon. I'll confess to you now — I wanted to go with you to Pheemy's to see if Granny was rebuilding the place. But once we were started, it was so pleasant and so much fun, I'm glad we took the drive."

"Whatever your motives," Judy said, "I'm glad we took the drive, too. I'm glad for another reason. When I first came to The Turrets, I thought you didn't like me very well . . . "

"I didn't know you."

"Yes. Isn't there an old saying — 'You can't like someone you don't know'?"

"Maybe. I'm thinking of a modern saying — or perhaps it's a song. To know her is to love her . . . "

Judy did not dare look at him and could think of nothing to say. She couldn't take exception to his choice of words because he might have meant nothing by them. On the other hand, if she made some flip remark, it would definitely sound rude. Judy kept silent, and Whit was apparently wrapped in his own thoughts. It was a relief to recognize familiar landmarks and to know The Turrets was not far away. As they turned into the driveway, Judy found her voice.

"Well, here we are!" The effort sounded feeble in her own ears. Whit echoed her words as he sent the car smoothly up the drive.

"Here we are . . . What the devil is that?"

He braked the car so abruptly Judy just saved herself from hitting the windshield. There was no need to ask what 'that' was. It was a huge statue of a Greek maiden in flowing draperies, balancing a water jar on one white shoulder. She was standing in a saucer-like basin edged with marble flowers, and below was a still larger saucer, rimmed not only with flowers, but adorned with cherubim whose hands were outstretched toward the center, as a child would reach out to feel falling raindrops.

"It's a fountain!" Judy said in a dazed voice.

"It's a monstrosity," said Whit in a voice so controlled it was hard to understand him. He drove the car over to one side and, without looking at Judy, went across the terrace and into the house like an avenging spirit. Judy was about to follow him, but curiosity got the better of her. She circled around and stood in front of the fountain, gazing up at the imperturbable maiden.

It was a tremendous fountain, fully twelve feet high; the lower basin was at least ten feet in diameter. The lines were graceful, the expressions of the cherubim adorable, and with water pouring from the water jug and splashing from one basin to another, it would be a beautiful sight. Upon closer inspection, Judy could see that the fountain was not new. Some of the flowers were chipped; one of the cherubim had lost a hand, and there were faint yellow streaks on the central column which were obviously rust stains that had been imperfectly removed.

Even so, although she was not an expert on fountains, Judy thought Melissa Beyer had probably gotten a bargain in buying the piece for twenty-five hundred dollars. But she was sure Whit would not think so. He would see no beauty in it whatever; instead he would see the fountain as a symbol of all the useless decoration so popular when The Turrets had been built and an extravagance which would climax for him the many extravagances he had tolerated in the household.

She was still standing looking up at the fountain when Whit banged out of the house, got into the convertible and zoomed away. He did not look in her direction, and Judy wondered if he had seen his grandmother. If he had . . . she ran suddenly across the terrace, afraid for her employer. Another stroke might be too much for even the intrepid Melissa Beyer . . .

But her fears were groundless, she saw at once as she came into the hall. Melissa was making her way toward the elevator, and her expression was serene, although she looked a little pale.

"I'm glad you're back, Judy; I need a massage tonight. How was Pheemy?"

"She was fine." Her visit to the expectant mother was so far in the background she had all but forgotten it. "We had a lovely drive, and we did get apples and squash . . . " Judy's voice trailed off as she realized they were still in the trunk of the car and probably would remain there or be thrown out by an enraged Whit.

Melissa Beyer smiled thinly. "My grandson left in a tearing hurry. He's gone to get Elaine Peavy and bring her back for a council of war," she said as they got into the elevator and Melissa pressed the button.

"You knew Whit wouldn't approve of the fountain," Judy said gently.

"Yes." Melissa walked into her ornate sitting room and went over to the bay window. She stood looking out, and Judy realized the fountain must be visible from where she stood. "But it *is* so pretty. Did I ever tell you my husband and I went to Rome on our honeymoon? The fountains are beautiful there. I always wanted one. This is really a bargain . . . "

Judy prepared her tray for the massage and reminded herself sternly she must not take sides. She felt she was permitted, however, to make one halfway approving remark.

"Two thousand dollars of the money was yours anyway," she said, "so I guess you can spend it for a fountain if you want to."

Melissa turned and came reluctantly toward the bed, and all at once she looked tired and old.

"I had a right to buy the fountain," she said slowly. "I believe Whitney — and even Elaine Peavy — will admit that. But I didn't realize one important thing — a fountain needs water. Jim, the gardener, tells me it will cost a horrible amount to install the pipes and outlets and motor and things, and I'll have to notify the town fathers about the water I'm going to use and pay extra for it . . . Oh, Judy! Whitney was terribly mad — actually in a rage. Do you think — is it possible — he would have me committed to an institution?"

Melissa Beyer's face suddenly crumpled and, like a child, she put her head on Judy's shoulder and sobbed unrestrainedly.

10

WHEN Elaine came into the living room that evening, looking extraordinarily lovely in an ice-blue sheath with a white cardigan slung around her shoulders, Judy was pleased to see the redhead's expression was, for a change, quite pleasant. She cocked an inquiring eye at her employer and whispered:

"It looks to me as if your future granddaughter-in-law likes fountains, too."

"I don't trust that woman," Melissa whispered back. But Judy noted with satisfaction that Mrs. Beyer's color was normal and that their quiet meal together before the fireplace in Melissa's bedroom had done a great deal to restore the older woman's poise and to ease her nervous tension.

Melissa Beyer had not again expressed

any fear that her grandson would have her judged mentally incompetent. After Judy had soothed her down and given her a brisk massage, she was restored to her usual determined self. But when she went down to the kitchen to arrange for a dinner tray with Katy, Judy got a clue to the tension which had been building in Melissa Beyer ever since the fountain had been delivered early in the afternoon.

Katy reported that she and Jim, the gardener, were both on the terrace when two huge vans drove up and a small army of workmen proceeded to uncrate the fountain and set it up under Melissa Beyer's direction.

Katy herself had thought the fountain very pretty, but Jim looked upon it sourly from the first. He said:

"'Why'd you want to go and get a fool thing like this for?'" repeated Katy, delighted to report the scene in detail. "Jim's been here so long he don't have the proper respect. I guess maybe he was mad, because he told Mrs. Beyer the pipe for the fountain would have to go right through that big bed of canna lilies. Then he started talking about how much it would cost and all, and of course Mis' Beyer got kinda upset."

"I guess it would cost quite a bit to set up a fountain as large as that," Judy commented. She was thinking it made very little difference, since Whit would probably never allow the fountain to be set up in any case.

"I was trying to tell Mis' Beyer that," Katy said, taking the lamb chops out of the broiler, and fixing up the plates for the tray. "She had some sort of idea she could have me cut down on kitchen expenses by using margarine instead of butter and not making so many pastries and things like that. But Lord love us, Miss Jordan, what you could save that way wouldn't pay for a foot of pipe for the fountain. Then Mis' Beyer said she will not have any more at homes — except that big one she's planned for Thanksgiving weekend. But I told her I didn't see why the fountain had to have water in it anyway. I think it looks pretty just as it is. I told her right out she was crazy to think of saving a few pennies here and there when Jim said the fountain connections and a pump and all might cost maybe close to a thousand dollars."

So that was where Melissa Beyer had gotten the idea that if Katy, the cook, thought she was acting in an erratic fashion, her grandson might have the same point of view! But, watching Whit Beyer as he came into the room after Elaine, Judy did not think this was on his mind at all. He looked like a thundercloud and made no attempt to conceal his rage. Usually he greeted his grandmother with a kiss and had a pleasant word for Judy. But this time he said nothing, and only Elaine's murmured hello as she took the wing chair opposite Mrs. Beyer broke the atmosphere of gloom that Whit had wrapped about himself like a cloak.

"I suppose there's no use beating

about the bush," Elaine said with a rueful laugh. "I've been telling Whit he should snap out of it. There's no sense getting mad at a fountain; perhaps it will even add to the value of the place when you decide to sell."

"Who said anything about selling?" demanded Melissa.

"I did," Whit said sharply. "I've said many times before that you must sell this place, Granny. It's like pouring money through a sieve keeping the place up. And now you add a fountain! Have you any idea how much it's going to cost just to install the darn thing?"

"Jim has been telling me all about it," Melissa said dryly. "But I figured out a way to save the money, Whitney. Katy can economize a great deal on the food, I'm sure, and Consuela won't need a special maid to help her; one girl can work both in the kitchen and upstairs. And I'll give up my at homes," she said with a note of triumph.

Elaine Peavy laughed merrily and

indulgently, as if Mrs. Beyer were a child who had said something clever. Judy fiercely resented her attitude, but she had to admit Melissa Beyer's position was indefensible. Whit did not even bother to answer his grandmother's suggestions.

"There's no use discussing how the fountain can be set up or how much it will cost," he said in a tone that brooked no argument. "If you could return it to the scoundrel who sold it to you and get your money back, I'd be willing to listen. But of course, since he's unloaded it, you'll never see him again. So forget the fountain. I'll have the place listed for sale with a real estate agent I know, and you'd better make up your mind where you want to live. If you don't like a nursing home, perhaps you would be comfortable in a small apartment or in one of those developments which they have for senior citizens . . . "

Melissa's snort effectively stopped Whit from pursuing the subject, and

Judy, glancing at her patient, felt it was time to take a hand.

"I'm sure your grandmother will find an interesting and stimulating life wherever she goes," she said smoothly. "But you must remember this is an important decision which cannot be made in a moment."

"You can't find a buyer in a moment either," said Elaine Peavy sarcastically.

"If I must sell this place, Whitney," Melissa Beyer said with a slight quaver in her voice, "I want to be sure it goes to someone who will appreciate it. This has been my home for many years, and no matter how far I go away from it, it will still be home in my heart. I couldn't bear to think of it being left to fall apart or getting sold to careless people who might deface the woodwork, for instance."

Elaine Peavy's face was fast regaining its customary expression of discontent, Judy noted, wondering at it. But Whit, with a businessman's logic, said to his grandmother:

"I don't know why you should care what happens to the place after you sell it. Perhaps the new owner might want to tear it down and put up a number of houses on this plot so that he could realize a good return on his investment."

Melissa Beyer shuddered. "I certainly wouldn't sell for any such purpose. I have my neighbors to think of."

"It would be an ideal spot for a supermarket," Elaine suggested, and Judy thought she spoke maliciously.

"If I might make a suggestion," she said quickly, before Melissa could become too angry, "there is a solution to the problem of selling this place to an individual or a group which would please everyone."

"Aren't you the bright one?" Elaine said sarcastically. "May I point out, Miss Jordan, that the disposition of Mrs. Beyer's estate is absolutely no concern of yours?"

Whitney silenced his fiancée with a glance. "I'd like to hear your suggestion, Judy. You are fairly level-headed, I know."

"At Park View Hospital," Judy said her cheeks pink with pleasure at Whit's compliment, "we discovered there is a real need for convalescent homes. Not many women are as fortunate as you are, Mrs. Beyer, in having a place where they can come and be taken care of while they recuperate from a severe illness. Even those who are able to pay a reasonable amount cannot get the nursing care they require if they try to establish themselves in an apartment. Very few families these days have living quarters large enough to take care of an extra person, and someone active enough and competent enough to take on the specialized care a convalescent needs simply doesn't exist in the usual setup."

"I never thought of that," Melissa Beyer commented.

"I suppose," Elaine said angrily, "if a buyer wanted to set up a convalescent home here, you would expect Whit and his grandmother to give the place away."

"No, I don't believe that would enter into it," Judy started to protest. But Whit interrupted:

"If a buyer were going to use this place for a convalescent home or a special school or anything of the sort, I don't know why we wouldn't compromise on the price. To my mind, it would be like giving a certain amount to charity."

"I would be entirely agreeable to selling the property if it could be used to benefit humanity," Melissa Beyer said, with a gleam in her eye puzzling to Judy but apparently clear to Elaine Peavy.

"You can afford to be generous," the redhead said, "in a theoretical case like this. May I point out, Whitney darling, that this property is going to be very difficult to unload, even at a sacrifice? The house is a perfect white elephant; I believe even a nursing home staff would have to do so much rebuilding they wouldn't be interested in the place. Yes, Miss Jordan, you have made the perfect suggestion. If someone can find a buyer for The Turrets who has not only enough money but is willing to spend his life and energy on a worthy cause, then your employer will be able to live here for many years to come. And you, of course, can keep your job."

Judy felt the hot blood rising to her face in a wave she was powerless to control. What Elaine said was perfectly true, of course. An old, inconvenient mansion set in acres of carefully landscaped grounds was a difficult piece of property to move. She had once heard Doctor Everett comment that sometimes owners of such property tried to give it away to escape the heavy tax load.

"Elaine, you shouldn't say things like that," Whitney said reprovingly. "Miss Jordan was only trying to be helpful, and I do feel Granny has a point, too. Usually, I believe, a buyer will tell you what he has in mind when he is negotiating for property. At any rate, it is foolish for us to discuss the matter between ourselves. All I want to get settled is that you will let me list the place with a real estate agent. Will you do that, Granny?"

"Yes, I will," His grandmother said, nodding placidly. "But I reserve the right to refuse to go through with the transaction unless I approve the purpose for which the house will be used. And I will never approve of selling to the man who wants to set up a supermarket," she added with a venomous glance at Elaine.

"Before you list the place with an agent, Whitney darling," Elaine said, as if the older woman had not spoken, "why don't you give me a chance to make a few inquiries? There is one man, for instance, who has bought quite a few things in my shop and for whom I have bought some antiques on commission. He might be interested in a place like this."

"Is he a good-looking fellow?" Whit demanded.

"Don't play the heavy jealous lover with me," Elaine said coldly. "What the man looks like has nothing to do with it; I am interested in the commission. A girl likes to have some money of her own when she gets married," Elaine added, dropping her lashes demurely.

Judy looked over at Mrs. Beyer, and her employer's face was bleak. It was obvious that no matter what obstacles she put in the way of completing the sale of the house, Elaine Peavy would manage somehow to overcome them. The redhead was not averse to acquiring a few thousand dollars by acting as agent in the sale. But her primary object probably was to marry Whitney Beyer. Judy felt an unreasonable pang of jealousy at the thought.

"Your grandmother has had a tiring day," she said now to Whit, who was gazing fondly at Elaine. "Perhaps we can continue this discussion another time."

Melissa Beyer got to her feet at once and stood leaning heavily on her cane.

"Judy is right," she said briskly. "I've had quite a bit of excitement, and anyway, it's close to my bedtime. I do want to ask one favor, Whit; I'd like to have my last at home on the Thanksgiving weekend. It will be a farewell party, in a way."

Whit agreed at once, and as Judy and Melissa left the room Judy knew Elaine would bend every effort to convince her fiancé that this one generous gesture was the last he should have to make for his grandmother.

"I want to thank you for your suggestion, Judy," Melissa Beyer said with a smile as Judy prepared to make her comfortable in bed. "It won't do any good, of course. Elaine Peavy will keep after Whit. A man can stand just so much nagging. Eventually Whit will give in and agree to whatever she says, regardless of my feelings."

Judy admitted, with a sigh, that this was so. "But there honestly is a need for more convalescent homes," she told her employer. "I think if you ask Doctor Everett, he will back me up. Elaine is too pessimistic about the need of extensive rebuilding in a house as beautifully kept up as this one has been since it was first built. I am sure it would cost much less to set up a nursing home in it than it would to rebuild on this or any other location."

"Why don't you go down to New York and ask Eph Everett about it?" Melissa said, on a sudden inspiration. "Who knows? He might even know of someone who is anxious to find just such a place as this."

"I'd like to talk with Doctor Everett," Judy said, "and I'll go the day after tomorrow, if that is all right with you."

"It's a good idea," Melissa Beyer said, smiling with satisfaction at the way her suggestion had been received.

"Actually, you can kill two birds with one stone. You'll have a chance to see someone while you are there, and after you've talked to Eph Everett I may be able to do Elaine Peavy out of a nice fat commission!"

11

JUDY approached the modern and impersonal façade of the Park View Hospital in New York with mingled feelings. She had not been away from it for a great length of time, but everything, including the flat, uninteresting face of the block-long building, seemed to show up with unusual clarity in the afternoon sunlight. Perhaps it was because she was now used to the many spires and minarets of The Turrets, the soft weathered stone of the building itself and the balconies with their wrought-iron railings, she told herself. But The Turrets was too old-fashioned to endure. A modern builder would take advantage of every inch of the space it occupied. Perhaps she could persuade Doctor Everett to help her employer sell the place to some individual or group who could make use of its charm as well as its size.

"My, we're looking blooming this afternoon," Doctor Everett commented as she came into his office. He was a short, heavy-set man with a shock of white hair and extraordinarily bushy white eyebrows. He was always meticulously clean, but he managed somehow to look untidy. His white coat, unbuttoned, flew behind him as he dashed down the hall, and he had a habit of running his hands through his hair that made it look as if he had just been out in a high wind.

"Thank you," murmured Judy, as she sank into the chair in front of his desk. "If I look well, it's because I enjoy the work. Mrs. Beyer is delightful."

"Ah, you should have seen her forty years ago," Doctor Everett said with a nostalgic sigh. "She was very beautiful, but more than that, she had great spirit. I often thought it a pity that Melissa Beyer, who could have led an army or run a crusade, confined her talents and her leadership to the small town of Greenmeadow. But of course that's all in the past. I understand that her grandson now wants to put her on the shelf. Melissa said you'd explain."

Judy, aware of how precious time was to the chief of staff of Park View Hospital, gave him a brief outline of the situation at The Turrets and told him how anxious Whitney Beyer was to sell before he married.

Doctor Everett listened with concentration, nodding his head from time to time. When Judy got to the point of explaining how Melissa felt about selling her home to someone who would use it for a dignified and worthwhile purpose, he sat silent for a few moments.

"I am glad Melissa asked my advice," he said finally. "But of course there is nothing I can do about it. The need for a convalescent home is always with us. But you understand, my dear Judy, I am not concerned with real estate. And even if I knew of a group who was planning to open a rest home, I doubt if I could recommend any particular spot. At least I would not do so."

"You do think it a good idea, don't you?" Judy asked.

"Yes, it's a wonderful idea. But that is as far as I can go toward endorsing a project of this nature."

"I was afraid you could not do any more," Judy told him, "and I am sure Mrs. Beyer will understand. But just before I left Greenmeadow something came up; perhaps you can give us some advice on that."

Judy tried to present the facts without prejudice, but she was afraid some skepticism crept into her voice. Before she left The Turrets, Melissa Beyer had had a phone call from Elaine Peavy. Elaine had found a man who was definitely interested in buying the place and had assured him that it would be at least a week before she could give him all the details.

"A week!" Melissa had echoed over the telephone. "I should hope so. Is this the man you were talking about — the one who buys all the antique furniture?"

It was a different man, Elaine Peavy had explained. He was a very fine person, and his idea was to open a school for children with speech defects. He was familiar with the location of The Turrets, and she was sure he would not haggle over price.

"What's his name?" Melissa had demanded, but her only answer had been a mocking laugh from Elaine.

Talking it over with her employer before she left for New York, Judy had agreed that Elaine had been very quick to find a buyer who met all specifications. It seemed almost incredible to Judy, as well as to Melissa, that the redhead had been able to locate a humanitarian who was engaged on a project which could make use of The Turrets so quickly. It was beyond belief!

"I've told you all this," Judy said now to Doctor Everett, "because I thought you might be able to give me the name of some man or group which is planning such a project, or looking for new quarters for an existing school of this type."

"A school for children with speech defects," said the doctor, moving the papers on his desk to form a new pattern, a habit of his, Judy knew, when he was thinking. "Let me see. I don't know of any group that fits," he added. "I'll make a few phone calls and see what I can find out. Meanwhile, you can run around and visit some of your old friends if you like. But don't be long. I have a conference coming up."

Judy made the rounds of her familiar tours of duty and listened avidly, as she was expected to do, to the latest news of the hospital personnel. But she did not want to keep Doctor Everett waiting and returned speedily to his office. He shook his head at her as she entered.

"I've called a lot of people who ought

to know the answer to your question," he told her, "but I haven't been able to turn up a clue. Somebody told me of a school of this type that is being organized in Europe, but arrangements for the site have already been completed. As far as I can find out, there's no such project in the works here."

"Well, it helps to have definite information on this subject. I can't thank you enough, Doctor Everett, for giving me so much time . . . "

She was interrupted by the telephone bell.

"For you," he said, handing the receiver to her. Instantly she was frightened. If anything had happened to Melissa Beyer while she was away . . . But it was Jock Campbell. Her relief was so great that her greeting was warmer than she meant it to be.

"How did you know where I was?" she asked after a moment.

"Mrs. Beyer told me," explained Jock. "I called the house to speak to her about Elaine's good news, and she mentioned you were seeing Doctor Everett in New York. It seemed like a good opportunity to take you to dinner, if I could catch up with you. So here I am on the phone. Shall I pick you up at the hospital in, say, half an hour?"

It would be a pleasant break in her routine, Judy realized. She had seen very little of Jock lately, but he could be a lot of fun when he was in the mood.

"Come along," she said, "in half an hour."

★ ★ ★

Jock had tickets for a Broadway hit, it turned out. He would have, Judy told herself. These Wall Street brokers!

"You haven't seen this show?" he asked her anxiously.

"I? *That* show? Why, it's been open only two weeks, and I've been at The Turrets longer than that. Besides, it's a fabulous hit; I understand only someone with a key to the United States mint can afford to buy tickets for it." Judy settled happily into the taxicab beside him.

They would have dinner first, Jock suggested, at one of those places that served a special dinner and guaranteed to whisk its patrons through various courses in time to make a Broadway theater curtain. After the play they might take in a night club, and Judy could get a late-late train for Springfield.

"I've taken the liberty to phone The Turrets and ask to have Jim meet the train at the station," said Jock. "All right with you?"

"Jim must be fuming," laughed Judy. "But yes, it's all right with me."

Jock apparently put himself out to be charming at dinner, Judy found. He took pains to encourage her to talk about her visit to Doctor Everett, and it was only the next day that she realized he had questioned her closely about what she had learned about a projected school for children with speech defects. She remarked Elaine seemed to be just plain lucky to have found an appropriate buyer for The Turrets with such phenomenal speed and wondered out loud that Doctor Everett had been unable to give her any information about it.

"It's quite a hush-hush affair, I understand," said Jock smoothly. "Elaine cautioned me to say nothing about it on the Street."

"Wall Street," explained Jock. "If the news got around it might — oh, you know — investors don't like to have one of their group mixed up in anything that might get publicity."

"I am puzzled," Judy said. "I thought we were talking about a school for children with speech defects. You seem to be talking about somebody in Wall Street, and I don't see the connection."

Jock looked at her with a grin and said:

"You are one of the original Babes

in the Wood. Elaine told me Melissa Beyer would not sell her place to anyone but a do-gooder. Am I right?"

"Yes, of course."

"So — I happen to know a man down in the Street who wants to buy a setup like The Turrets: a big place, in a respectable neighborhood, with enough ground to keep the neighbors from being nosy, not too far from New York. I didn't want to enter into it myself, so I told the guy to get in touch with Elaine."

"So you are really the one who found the buyer for the place!"

"You're catching on, Baby. I don't mind Elaine getting the commission; I've known her for a long time, and she and I have worked on a couple of deals before . . . "

"Does your friend really intend to start a remedial school?" Judy asked carefully.

Jock laughed and, as usual, he looked far less homely.

"Not by a long shot. That was a

bright idea of Elaine's to get Melissa's signature on the dotted line."

"Have you told Whit about this?"

"No. And I wouldn't advise you to tell him either." Jock's expression was no longer amused. "In fact, this whole conversation, my dear Judy, is off the record. You are not going to mention it to Whit, to his grandmother or to Peter Baylis."

"What has Peter to do with it?" Judy asked.

"You're behind the times," Jock said impatiently. "Melissa has already been in touch with your boy friend and has asked him to handle the legal part of the sale for her. I gather you didn't tell your fiancé you were coming to New York?"

"I didn't think I would have time to see him," Judy stammered.

"Good. Then you can keep a secret when you want to."

"I will not be a party to any such deceitful transaction," Judy said with spirit. "Melissa Beyer is a kind and good woman. If she wants to sell her house so that it can be used to help others, I don't think you should interfere."

"Oh, grow up!" exclaimed Jock. He looked more than homely; he looked positively ugly. "If Melissa wants to set up a remedial school or open a convalescent home, she ought to give the place away. I notice she's not doing that. She wants a bit of cash just like the rest of us. And if she sells to a buyer — any buyer — she must abide by the terms of the sale. She cannot dictate the purpose for which the house is to be used."

"But she can refuse to sell," Judy said triumphantly. "And after I tell her . . . "

"You will tell her nothing," Jock said, and there was a steely quality in his voice Judy had never heard before. "In the first place I would deny I had said anything at all about the sale; in fact, like a gentleman, I would deny having seen you while you were in New

York. Of course no one would believe me," he added as Judy made a gesture of protest. "But then it would be all the more convincing. Your employer and Whit and your fiancé, Peter Baylis, would think you had dreamed up this conversation so that you wouldn't have to tell them what we really talked about or did tonight."

"You wouldn't be so despicable," Judy said with a confidence she did not feel.

"You don't know me very well," Jock retorted. He was smiling, but his eyes were cold. "Anyhow, perhaps I'd better warn you: my friend who is interested in The Turrets doesn't like little girls who go around blabbing about his business deals. It makes him nervous."

"You make *me* nervous," Judy said, with an attempt to sound sarcastic. "You're talking about your friend as if he were a gangster, as if he wanted to buy The Turrets for a hideaway or something."

"You don't have to worry about it," Jock said shortly.

"Yes, I do," Judy contradicted. "Melissa Beyer is my friend as well as my employer. If you didn't expect me to be loyal to her, just why did you tell me all this in the first place?"

"Because I don't want you to put any spokes in any wheels," Jock said threateningly. "I want you to be a good little girl, and when you go back to The Turrets you just report that Doctor Everett said he would look into the expanding field for new schools in remedial subjects. You don't have to report that he knows who is going to buy the place. You don't have to do any lying. All you have to do with the old lady is stall her along until we get that signature on the deed."

"But won't Peter know who the buyer is if he draws up the papers for the sale?" Judy questioned.

"The name will mean nothing to him, because he will deal only with my friend's lawyer. And my friend's lawyer, by the way, will not talk about what his client is going to do with the property. As I told you, if Mrs. Beyer sells, she has nothing further to say about it. The only time she can dictate what will happen to that house or on that property is if she gives the whole place away."

"But if I tell her what your friend plans to do . . . "

"Do you know what he's going to do?"

"No."

"Then you can't say anything one way or another, can you? Of course you can make her suspicious and reluctant to sell. But I repeat, my dear Judy, it would not be wise for you to stir up any trouble. Just say that Doctor Everett is looking into the matter, and Elaine and I will take it from there."

"And if I refuse?" questioned Judy. "If I decide to tell Melissa all about this, what can your friend do about it?"

Jock shook his head at her reprovingly.

"I don't think you will be so foolish," he told her. "I must ask for your promise not to say anything and not to do anything. Otherwise, in order to protect my friend's interests, I will see to it you have a little difficulty getting back to Greenmeadow tonight. After the show, I will offer to drive you home. We will break down on some lonely country road. Or we might elope. At any rate, something will happen to keep you away from The Turrets for a couple of days and perhaps convince you you should have listened to me in the first place."

"I don't care what you do with me," Judy said defiantly. "You'll have to take me back eventually, and whenever I get to The Turrets I'll tell Mrs. Beyer she is being tricked into this sale."

Jock laughed, although there was no merriment in his voice. "You can talk away after we've been driving around for a couple of days," he said indifferently. "Nobody will believe you. Now, do I get that promise?"

Judy felt trapped. She had no doubt Jock Campbell meant what he said and would tolerate no interference with his plans. She would have to promise to do as he asked and trust to luck there would be some way she could warn Melissa or Whit that they were becoming involved in a criminal proceeding.

12

IT was just as well she had not arrived at The Turrets until three o'clock in the morning, Judy thought as she looked at herself in the mirror the next morning. There were dark circles beneath her eyes, and her hair looked lifeless and dull. She did the best she could with make-up, but she was almost prepared for Melissa's comment when she walked into the bedroom:

"New York certainly doesn't agree with you, Judy. You either had a very gay time, or else you had a very difficult session with Doctor Everett. Did that old coot want you to come back to work for him?"

"No," said Judy, smiling with an effort. "My session with Doctor Everett was quite disappointing, but he said nothing about me leaving The Turrets.

I am a little tired; Jock Campbell took me to dinner and to a play afterward, and the train was delayed right outside New Haven, so I didn't get much rest."

In spite of all her efforts, Judy could not bring herself to tell her employer a deliberate lie about what Doctor Everett had said. She waited for Melissa to start the discussion, and finally the older woman asked:

"What did Eph say that was so disappointing? Do you think I'd better hold off on the sale of the house until we find out more about this buyer Elaine has lined up?"

"Oh, no," Judy said, too quickly. Melissa Beyer raised her eyebrows but made no comment as Judy stumbled on. "I mean — Doctor Everett didn't know of any group starting a remedial school right away, in this country, at least . . . But of course he could hear about somebody at any time . . . I mean if he inquires around . . . "

"I know what you mean," Melissa

said dryly. "I think perhaps you are overtired by your trip to New York, and there is nothing further to be discussed anyway at this time. I asked Peter Baylis to come here and stay overnight. Elaine said something about having a check which will be held in escrow, as I understand it. But all that can wait until you get rested. In the meantime, Consuela and I are going to go over some of the clothes I have in the attic to see what can be disposed of to the Salvation Army. I should have cleared out the place long ago, no matter whether I was selling the house or not."

"Did Elaine tell you the name of the man who was going to buy the place?" Judy said as she turned to go.

"No, just the name of the lawyer, a Mr. Feathergill. I never heard of him, myself. Why do you ask?"

"No reason," Judy said, and escaped to her own room.

★ ★ ★

It was a peculiar day, cold and dreary outside. Jim built a fire in her fireplace, and Katy, who had apparently been told Mrs. Beyer was not feeling well, sent up a tray at noon. But Judy knew she would have to appear at dinner, and somehow she would have to act as if she did not know how Melissa was being tricked into the sale. When she went down to the living room, however, things were made unexpectedly easy. Whit and Elaine were there, and it was obvious the redhead was feeling on top of the world. She greeted Judy nonchalantly, and whether or not she knew how much Jock had said, she did not appear worried about it.

"Mr. Feathergill says he already has the check from the buyer," Elaine was telling Whitney as Judy came into the room. "Isn't that marvelous?"

"You should be very pleased," Whitney commented, smiling down at her. "This check is called 'earnest money,' and usually the whole thing goes to the person who arranged the sale — as a commission. In this case, that person is you."

"It is, you know!" Elaine crowed, dancing gaily around the room and snapping her fingers.

"Didn't Jock Campbell have anything to do with it?" asked Judy.

Elaine Peavy stopped her impromptu dance as if she had been slapped, and Whit looked at Judy curiously.

"I am handling the sale of this house," Elaine said in a hard voice. "Whatever Jock Campbell said to you — forget it."

"What are you getting excited about?" Whit demanded. "She only asked . . ."

"I know what she said," Elaine snapped. "She's trying to imply I didn't earn the commission. I don't see that it's any of your business, Miss Jordan, beyond the fact, of course, that you'll be out of a job the minute the sale goes through."

"I'm sorry if I made you angry," Judy began, but Whit interrupted:

"Drop it, Elaine. You're making a

mountain out of a molehill."

Elaine looked at Whit and smiled. Then she went over and, standing close to him, playfully tweaked his ear.

"Don't you know why I'm so nervous and edgy, darling?" she asked. "It's because once the house is sold and your grandmother has decided where she wants to go, we can make our plans for an early marriage."

"Did somebody say marriage?" Peter Baylis asked, striding into the room. He walked over to Judy and kissed her soundly. "Not that you deserve a kiss, my pet," he told her severely, "but I just can't seem to help myself when you're around."

As usual, Elaine Peavy reacted to the sight of a man, especially one who was young and attractive. Assuming a Western drawl, she called Judy 'Podner' and asked for a 'knockdown.' Judy hastily made the introductions, and Whit shook hands in something less than a cordial manner. Judy had not realized that Peter's brief visit to The

Turrets had not been known to Elaine and Whit. She hastily explained Peter was there at the invitation of Mrs. Beyer, and that as a lawyer he would handle the papers for Whit's grandmother when the house was sold.

"The sale is most important to all of us," Elaine said, looking archly at Peter. "When you came in, I was telling Whit now we can plan to get married during the holidays."

"Congratulations," Peter said, nodding at Whit. "I'm hopeful Judy and I can make definite plans now. You know, darling," he said to Judy, "an opportunity I had to go to the West Coast has come up sooner than I expected. I wanted your decision by Thanksgiving, but if you could make up your mind sooner, we could make it a honeymoon trip."

"Well, now," Whit said, glancing at Judy's troubled face, "perhaps we'd better get the sale of the house settled first before any of us makes definite plans."

"This is a switch!" Elaine said with mock indignation. "You've been the one who wanted me to set the date, and now, when Peter asks Judy to do the same thing, you think he ought to wait. Pay no attention to him," she advised Peter. "He's got the on-the-way-to-the-church jitters."

"But he's quite right, Elaine," Judy protested. "The sale of the house is most important." She broke off as she heard Melissa's cane in the hall and went out to help her employer into the room and to get her seated in her usual chair by the fireplace. Judy could feel the excitement that made her employer's arm quiver as she guided her to the chair. But Melissa Beyer was a past master at concealing her feelings, and Judy knew nothing would hurry her employer in any case.

Melissa's brittle manner continued all through dinner. The meal was served in the morning room, and privately Judy thought it a far more attractive place to eat than the big gloomy dining room had ever been. The oval drop-leaf table provided ample seating space for the five of them, and Katy had assured her there were enough extra leaves so the table could accommodate eight or ten. When the house had been built, the room had been given an extra quota of windows in addition to the three in the turret at one corner. It was always bright and cheerful at night; with the candles lit on the table and the wall sconces glowing against the soft blue of the walls, it made a charming and informal family dining room.

Only, Judy thought, looking around the table, they were anything but a united family. Melissa, although she was a perfect hostess as always, was obviously under a strain. Whitney was apparently disturbed by what Elaine had said to Judy, and Judy herself felt helpless to rise above the gloom of her own thoughts.

But Peter Baylis noticed no constraint. Judy had never admired him more than she did during the next hour, when he chattered on about the court cases which had come to his notice and which were usually interesting enough to be considered items of news.

"Do you work on murder cases?" Elaine Peavy asked, as Peter finished an anecdote.

"No." Peter smiled. "My work is what you might call dull. It's concerned with corporation law, real estate, wills and things like that."

"You say it's dull," Judy said, and her voice was warm with gratitude toward him for carrying off a difficult situation so well. "But it isn't dull to you. You get more excited over a clause in a contract than any other lawyer would get if he had to prove who murdered whom and where and when."

"I'm delighted to see a young man enjoying his work," Melissa Beyer said. "It seems to be the fashion nowadays for anyone who is working to discredit his job and to find it not only difficult but uninteresting. Not you, of course,

Whitney dear," she added hastily.

"Very few men have my opportunities," Whit said. "It's no credit to me that I enjoy the work. My father started a factory," he explained to Peter, "which has been adapted to making electronic parts. Naturally, I find the work challenging."

"You are always looking toward the future in that line," Peter agreed. "My work of necessity is largely concerned with what has been done in the past — precedent, you know."

"For that reason I am sure you will be able to give Granny good advice in arranging the sale of this place . . ."

"Whit dear, I would prefer to wait until after dinner to discuss the sale."

Judy, trying to think of something to bridge the awkward moment, said quickly:

"I don't believe you've seen the beautiful fountain Mrs. Beyer bought, Peter. If there's a moon, I'll show it to you after dinner . . ."

"I would prefer not to discuss the fountain either," Melissa Beyer said sharply.

"In that case," said Elaine, with a glance which showed how much she enjoyed Judy's discomfiture, "we'd better go back to your court cases, Peter. Are there any juicy scandals on the docket now?"

Peter obliged by again mentioning a case of more than passing interest. But although Melissa had been mollified, Judy knew that Whitney and Elaine as well as herself were curious as to what Melissa Beyer's announcement was going to be.

But at last the dinner hour was over and Judy once more helped her employer to the chair beside the fireplace. She was reminded again of the younger generation's comment that Melissa Beyer used her cane as a sceptre. The autocratic white-haired woman had never looked more regal than she did at that minute. However, Elaine Peavy was unimpressed. She did

203

not sit down but glanced at her wrist watch as she said:

"I'm sorry to rush you, my dear Mrs. Beyer, and I don't like to eat and dash away, but I am expecting an important phone call, and I have to get back to town by nine o'clock."

"By all means run along," Melissa Beyer said in the manner of one dismissing a lady-in-waiting. "I wouldn't want you to miss your phone call."

"Well, I really have nothing much to say," Elaine said, smiling a trifle nervously; "just that Mr. Feathergill already has the earnest money and I have his card here." She fumbled in her purse, found the card and held it out to Melissa Beyer. "I imagine you'll want Peter to get in touch with him . . . "

"No, I don't," Melissa Beyer said coolly, although she took the card. "Perhaps you'd better sit down for a minute after all, Elaine. You know, after Judy went to New York and saw Doctor Everett I became increasingly dissatisfied with what he had told her. It was exactly nothing!"

"What difference does that make?" Elaine demanded. "Just because your doctor friend never heard of the man who's going to buy your place, I don't see any reason for you to get all excited. After all, his money is as good as anyone else's."

"Elaine, you can't talk that way to Granny," Whit said harshly.

"It's all right, Whitney," Melissa Beyer said, although her eyes were sharp as she looked at the redhead. "I can understand Elaine's disappointment at losing a sale. But she knew I had agreed to sell only to a buyer who would use the place to promote a worthy cause."

"Do you want any more worthy cause than a school to help children correct speech defects?" Elaine asked sarcastically.

"But Doctor Everett explained to me none of the authorities in this field has any knowledge of such a school being set up in this part of the country."

Melissa's voice was calm, but it had a steely quality Judy had never heard before. "Since the buyer you found is evidently lying about the purpose for which he will use The Turrets, I have changed my mind about selling, at least to him."

"But you can't do that," Elaine said in a shocked voice. "You've already agreed to sell. Tell her, Whit."

Whitney looked at his grandmother with a troubled expression. "Aren't you making a hasty decision, Granny? Perhaps Doctor Everett hasn't heard about this latest project."

"I'm sure he would have heard," Melissa said firmly. "Isn't that so, Judy?"

"Yes — yes," Judy stammered. "Doctor Everett phoned a friend of his who is one of the leading authorities in the east on corrective speech therapy."

"I don't care!" Elaine cried in a shrill voice. "You can't change your mind now. The sale is all set."

"Have you signed anything?" Peter

said quietly to Melissa. When she shook her head, he said directly to Elaine: "Nothing is all set in the sale of property until you have the owner's signature."

"And you haven't got that," Melissa said with satisfaction. "You'll just have to find another buyer, Elaine, if you want your commission."

Elaine was so white with rage, Judy thought she might strike out at Whit, who had risen to his feet to stand beside her, and now put his hand under her elbow. Elaine pulled away, turned on her heel and without a word marched out of the room.

13

JUDY drove Peter to the train after breakfast the next morning and dutifully kissed him goodbye at the station. There had seemed to be no point in having him linger, since Melissa had been adamant about refusing to consider the buyer Elaine had found. Judy herself had felt a little sick at the thought of what Jock Campbell and his gangster friend might do, but she had decided against saying anything to Peter about it. In any case, he did not appear to consider the sale of the property of any importance in their personal life.

"You know, darling," he said, holding her shoulders in his strong hands so that she was forced to look into his eyes, "you can waste your life worrying about other people's problems. I agree Mrs. Beyer is a charming old woman.

I was wrong about her; she is kind and considerate. But still she is only your employer. Eventually she will find a buyer for The Turrets who will meet her specifications, and then the job will be over for you."

"But someone told me Mrs. Beyer couldn't dictate what was to be done with the place unless she gave it away as a gift. Is that true, Peter?"

"If you want a legal opinion, I would have to know a few more details," Peter said. "But just offhand, I should say it was true. If Mrs. Beyer wants to give the property to a group who would use it to promote a school for speech defects or medical research or anything else, the purpose can be so specified in the contract, and the recipient would be bound to observe the terms of the contract except for unforeseen circumstances, in which case he might be penalized or the property might revert to the former owner. But I don't know why we're talking about the sale of the property again," Peter said impatiently. "I want to talk about us."

"If I were the type of person who could just walk out of a situation and leave loose ends dangling all over the place, I don't believe you would want to marry me, Peter."

"You went away from New York and left a lot of loose ends dangling," Peter reminded her. "And one of those loose ends was me."

"Peter, that isn't true," Judy protested. "I wanted to get away to have time to think . . . Oh, here's your train! Well, never mind; I'll call you in a couple of days."

Peter's kiss was only a perfunctory peck. "Yes, call me up — better make it tomorrow. I'll have to let them know about going to the Coast."

Judy stood waving and looking after the train even after it had vanished far down the track and around the bend. Then she went slowly downstairs and walked to the parking lot where she had left Melissa's car. She wished she had been able to talk to Peter about Jock Campbell and the threat he had made if she 'interfered with the sale.' But Peter was too far removed from life at The Turrets. Judy wondered as she drove back to the house if Peter would not always be far removed from her immediate problems.

Judy went directly to her room when she returned to The Turrets; the day stretched ahead of her endlessly. Melissa Beyer probably thought she could carry on as usual until a suitable purchaser for the property was found. But would Whit stand for that? Wouldn't the empty fountain on the lawn be a constant reminder of the need for a decision? How could she possibly make up her mind about Peter when the problem of her job and Mrs. Beyer's future had to be solved first?

Although she seldom used rouge, Judy applied a touch of it to each cheek and was pleased to see it made her look a little better. No matter what her inner turmoil, she had been engaged to see that Melissa Beyer did not suffer any ill effects from scenes such as the one of the previous night, and she had to present a calm and placid manner to her employer. She left the room reluctantly and stepped out into the hall; it would have been pleasant to relax quietly for even fifteen minutes.

Her room was at the front part of the house, and the windows in the hall looked out on trees whose glorious color was dimmed now. It was a short hall, bordering her room and the bath next door. At the end a door led directly into Mrs. Beyer's bed-sitting-room — a door Judy left open during the night so she could hear if her employer called.

"Did Peter catch his train all right?" Melissa asked. She was sitting behind her desk with many papers spread out before her. Some of them looked like legal documents, and Judy guessed her employer had been totaling up her assets and liabilities. She looked a little feverish, although her voice was composed.

"The train was on time," Judy said. She glanced over at the empty breakfast tray and asked: "Shall I take your tray down?"

"Later." Melissa swept the papers before her back into the strongbox. "I want to enjoy my moment of triumph over that sour-faced Elaine. But I suppose I'll have to give in eventually. Do you think Whitney will be very angry at me for changing my mind?"

"It's a woman's privilege, isn't it, to change her mind?" Judy tried to inject a gay note into her voice.

"Yes, I suppose so. I guess I can't put off leaving this house, much as I hate to. It isn't the same, anyway. If I can't have my fountain without making Whitney angry and if I have to give up my at homes, with Elaine waiting like a vulture to see if each one is the last . . . "

There was a knock on the door to

213

the hall, and the 'iron woman' looked inside. Her expression was worried.

"Pardon me, Mis' Beyer; did you want to get dressed now?"

"Yes, I suppose so," Melissa said with unaccustomed crossness. "We might as well get it over with, I guess." She reached for her cane and, bracing herself against the desk, started around it. Judy, watching her closely, saw her waver and close her eyes for a second. Instantly she was at Melissa's side, her arm around her waist.

"You're not doing anything but going back to bed," she said authoritatively. "Take the tray back to the kitchen, please, Consuela. Now, Mrs. Beyer, walk slowly. Sit here in this chair for a minute, and I'll straighten up your bed."

"Oh, Mis' Beyer, don't have another stroke," Consuela begged, but at a warning glance from Judy she picked up the tray and fled.

"I'm not going to have another stroke," Melissa said tartly. "I got a little dizzy there for a minute."

"And you were a little dizzy this morning, I imagine, when you got out of bed," Judy said, tightening the bed sheet.

"I often am," Melissa said airily. "I suppose I should take one of my pressure pills."

"You suppose right," Judy said cheerfully. "I'll get one for you. Now into bed. I'll give you a light back rub, and then you can nap for a while."

"Thank you, Judy." Melissa Beyer stretched out on the bed for a minute. "But even if I fall asleep, you must wake me in an hour. I want to drive out to see Pheemy."

"Pheemy isn't having her baby until next week," Judy said, rubbing her employer's back with gentle pressure. "The last time we were out there she was doing fine. Dick certainly cleaned up around the yard, too. The place looked much neater."

"Pheemy worried me," Mrs. Beyer said, slipping into the fresh nightgown

Judy held for her. "You and Doctor Everett between you have made a new person out of Pheemy. She's no longer a scared rabbit, she's a healthy young woman and looks forward to having her baby, as she should."

"Take your pill," Judy commanded, holding a glass of water ready. "I did very little. But of course Doctor Everett is wonderful. He stopped in to see Pheemy only once, but he changed her whole attitude toward being a mother."

"Shouldn't we worry anyhow?" Melissa asked drowsily. "The child may feel good, but she's all alone there, with no telephone. If she's working around when the baby starts to come, she won't be able to get help."

"Don't fret about it," Judy commanded. "After the emotional upset you've had these last few days, you simply must take care of yourself. I'm sure Pheemy is just fine, but to set your mind at ease, I'll drive out to see her. Okay?"

"Yes, I guess I'd better rest," Melissa agreed, closing her eyes. "Probably she's fine, but with a first baby, you never know."

Judy was satisfied her employer would stay in bed, but to make doubly sure she asked Consuela to stay with Melissa while she slept and on no account to let her get up until Judy returned.

It was good to have something to do, Judy reflected as she sent the car skimming along the road. It was a lowering day, with a sharp wind that whipped the leaves from the trees and swirled them in dusty piles. The afternoon she had driven with Whitney to see Pheemy had been bright, and the trees had been lovely. How long ago it seemed! She resolutely turned her mind from the memory of Whit saying softly: "To know her is to love her . . . "

She must give Peter his answer. There was no real doubt as to his love for her. If his manner was a little less than romantic, if his attitude and his actions could always be predicted, was that bad? If he was more excited about the new opportunity he had been offered on the Coast than he was about getting married, wasn't that a good sign? Peter was a lawyer; he was trained to think things over carefully and not to act on impulse. He was naturally orderly and tidy; perhaps they were not lovable qualities in themselves, but life could be smooth and placid with Peter.

Judy turned off onto the secondary road leading to Pheemy's farm and slowed down. The road was in need of repair, but it was only about two miles farther on . . . Too bad Pheemy didn't have any neighbor closer than the house she was passing. The chimney of the Ferris farm could be seen in the distance, but still it was too far to walk. Involuntarily Judy stepped on the gas and in a few minutes had to slow down again to turn into the Ferris drive.

She turned into the rutted roadway, and her heart as well as the car stopped!

Pheemy was in the road on her hands and knees, crawling toward her!

Judy pulled on the brake and was out of the car in one movement. Pheemy looked up, her eyes bright with pain and her face swollen and streaked with crying.

"The baby's coming, Nurse. It's coming right away. I can't stay here alone . . . Aahhh!" Pheemy's swollen figure jerked spasmodically and she lay down on the road, crying helplessly. "Help me — oh, help me!"

Judy reach down and took both the girl's hands in her own. "Hold tight, Pheemy. *Tight!* The pain will pass in a second. Take a deep breath. There! We've got to get you out of here."

Leaving Pheemy where she was, panting and exhausted, Judy got into the car, turned around and backed toward where she lay. Then, murmuring encouragingly, she helped Pheemy the few steps to the car, reached into the back seat for the blanket Melissa kept there and in a matter of seconds was back in the car and sending it flying down the road.

"Brace yourself against the seat; the road is bumpy, Judy warned. "When did the pains start?"

"A little while ago. I thought first it was only because I fell . . . "

"You *fell*!"

"I was putting up new kitchen curtains . . . Dick got them for me . . . I slipped off the chair . . . not hurt . . . " Pheemy said jerkily. She was perspiring, and Judy handed her a handkerchief. The pain would be coming soon again; Judy glanced at Pheemy and surprised a look of resolution on the young face.

"Sorry to be so much trouble, Nurse. I can hold out, I guess." her face contorted for a second, and she added: "Only hurry — hurry . . . "

Judy swung onto the highway, her mind mentally clocking the ten miles to the hospital. She could never make it with this traffic unless some miraculous hand swept the big trucks out of her path.

As if in answer to her unspoken prayer, a state police car came toward them in the opposite lane. While it was still far ahead, Judy put her hand on the horn and held it there. At the same time she swung around the truck ahead and shot forward, her foot pressing the gas pedal to the floor.

From then on, for Judy, everything happened almost as if she, the state troopers, the truck drivers and all the other drivers were actors in a play. She took her hand off the horn, but the drivers immediately ahead of her on the four-lane highway swung over to the right as soon as they could and cleared the center lane for her. Then, in her rear-view mirror, she saw the troopers' car make a U-turn and come after her. She slowed down slightly and swung the car over.

Pheemy was slumped forward, her head hanging. Judy glanced at her; there was nothing in her position to indicate the desperate need for haste to the troopers in the car following.

Yet she did not dare slow down. What could she do? Perhaps her horn . . . ?

Judy could not remember what the standard S.O.S. signal was; she had to take a chance. As the troopers came nearer she began to sound the horn: one blip, pause, two blips, pause, one blip. She repeated it again as the blue closed the gap between them. Then, as they drew alongside, she again pressed the horn in the staccato pattern. The car ahead of her had edged over as far as possible to the right, but still she had to slow down. She looked appealingly at the troopers.

Suddenly a blue-clad arm shot out of the window on her side and made the traditional sweeping gesture to urge her to follow them forward. At the same time the wailing siren screamed its warning, and the troopers shot ahead. Judy wrenched her car into the lane at her left and stepped on the gas. They had understood!

The miraculous hand she had wanted might have come down from the sky.

There were no cars in the lane ahead of the troopers; they melted to the right as if by magic, and Judy passed them as if they were standing still. There was no time to look at Pheemy; it took all her concentration to keep the light car hurtling forward at a speed she had never driven at before. The siren wailed on, rising and falling. Then, as they approached the cutoff to the hospital, it rose to an anguished scream that beat against the eardrums with nerve-shattering force.

Even so, the troopers had to slow down a little, and Judy perforce followed suit. But it was all right now, she thought, letting out her breath with a sigh. Just the next block, and one more, turn into the sweeping drive, brake to a stop — and they were there!

After the attendants had taken Pheemy inside, Judy let herself be helped into the waiting room by one of the troopers, a big, ruddy-faced fellow who was grinning at her sympathetically as she sat down.

"I guess you feel kind of all in," he said, taking out a notebook. "If you'll give me the name of the lady in the delivery room and some other details . . ."

Judy took out her wallet with her driver's license and gave him the information he wanted. At the end of the corridor a glass door gave a glimpse of a coffee shop, and it seemed to her nothing would be more heavenly than to get a cup of coffee, black and scalding hot. The trooper grinned again as he put the notebook away and turned to go.

"Thank you for everything," said Judy getting to her feet. "I'm so grateful you understood my odd signal with the horn. I didn't want to stop to explain."

"You made it clear enough you were in trouble, ma'am," the trooper assured her, "and then when I saw the woman next to you, I caught on real quick."

"But how did you know?" asked Judy. "I mean Pheemy was only

slumped over. I didn't know if you could even see her . . . "

"Maybe it was my intuition, ma'am," said the trooper. "I've got four of my own, and there's a fifth on the way. I hope the little tyke will be all right now. He had a rough ride."

He touched his cap and was gone. Judy made her way to the lunch counter and the coffee was as wonderful as she had thought it would be. Then she phoned Melissa and told her what had happened. Her employer agreed that she ought to wait at the hospital until the baby was born, even if that took some time.

But it was actually less than an hour later when the nurse came and told Judy the baby had arrived and both mother and child were doing well. She took down the information on how to reach the father, and then Judy called Melissa.

"How does it feel to be a new godmother?" she asked jubilantly. "A fine, healthy seven-and-half-pound baby girl!"

"I feel very proud," Mrs. Beyer said with a catch in her voice.

"Then you'd better get busy picking out a christening robe," Judy said briskly. "It will be needed when Melissa Beyer Ferris makes her formal debut!"

14

THE training and experience of a registered nurse had not rendered her immune to tension, Judy found. Pheemy's critical situation had taxed her nerves. The realization that, thanks to her, the girl had come safely and even triumphantly through the crisis did little to mitigate Judy's sensation of being tired and overwrought. When she reached The Turrets, she decided she had to get to bed at once.

She stopped in the kitchen where Katy was still at work clearing up after dinner and was warmly welcomed by the kindly cook. A plate of roast beef with mashed potatoes and new peas appeared from the warming oven, but Judy shook her head.

"Tea and one of your biscuits, Katy, is all I want," she said. "I'm dead on my feet."

Katy made sympathetic noises, but no one else's feelings could distract her from the enthralling topic of Pheemy's baby.

"Who does it look like?" she wanted to know. "How much does it weigh? Has she got any hair? And to think you found poor little Pheemy — she isn't more than a baby herself — all alone and in agony . . . "

For the third time Judy recounted what Pheemy had said when she found her; told how the fall had brought on labor before it was expected, how brave Pheemy had been through the wild ride to the hospital, how understanding the state troopers had been.

It was after nine o'clock before Judy could get away from the kitchen. In the game room she found Melissa Beyer practicing a trick shot at the billiard table and seemingly in high spirits. She looked guilty for a moment when Judy appeared, and was obviously relieved to hear that it was all right for her to stay up if she did not overtax herself.

"I feel good," Melissa said, waving her billiard cue to emphasize her words. "Not only do I have a new goddaughter, but Whitney is no longer angry with me. He told me this afternoon while you were away that he thought Elaine had been too hasty in arranging the sale. The dear boy doesn't want me to feel I am being rushed out of my home. As a matter of fact, I believe he's angry with Elaine now." She chuckled. "Anyway, he's gone down to see her and says he's going to call for a showdown."

Judy's head was spinning. With a final admonition to Mrs. Beyer to let Consuela help her to bed, she went up to her own room. It had never looked so inviting. She established some sort of record, she thought, undressing and getting ready for bed. She did remember to leave the door of her room into the hall open, and she opened the door of Mrs. Beyer's room too, certain that Consuela would leave it ajar if that was the way she found it. But she was so weary she wondered if even Gabriel's horn would have the power to wake her before she had had many hours of sleep.

When she did awaken Judy had a sense that something was wrong, dreadfully wrong. Had Mrs. Beyer rung her bell? Had someone called her? Perhaps she had heard the telephone in the downstairs hall. The waves of sleep rose around her again and threatened to engulf her.

Glancing at the illuminated dial of the clock on her bedside table, Judy saw it was only two-thirty. She snuggled into the pillow again with a sigh of relief, and then suddenly, as if someone had touched cold fingers to the back of her neck, she was wide awake, every sense alert. It was not noise which had roused her, she knew now; it was an odor. Was it — could it be — smoke?

Judy jumped out of bed and padded swiftly out to the hall, where a dim night light burned. The faint odor was stronger there, and as she looked toward her employer's half open door she thought she could see a slight shadow. It might be only her imagination. Judy snatched up a robe, stepped into her slippers and went swiftly into Melissa's room. Another night light glowed near the elevator door, and underneath that door little curls of smoke were seeping through, to spread and dissipate themselves over the flowered carpet. Judy pressed the switch near the door, and the room sprang into brilliant light. On the bed the elderly woman was stretched out, still asleep — or unconscious.

"Mrs. Beyer! Mrs. Beyer! Wake up!" Judy seized Melissa's shoulder with a gentle but urgent touch. She must not frighten her patient, but there was no time to lose. Melissa Beyer stirred and opened her eyes. She looked at Judy without comprehension.

"Mrs. Beyer! Melissa! Do you hear me?"

The older woman's eyes were closing again.

"Melissa! Don't go to sleep again. You must wake up! You must get up! Melissa, do you hear me?"

Judy tapped the elderly woman gently, first on one cheek and then on the other, talking to her and calling to her at the same time. She did not know how long the fire had been burning, nor how much smoke Melissa had already inhaled. But she had to get her employer out of bed and out into the hall, at least. It would do no good to call for help. Whitney's rooms were on the other side of the big house. Consuela and Katy were sleeping in the kitchen wing, also too far away to be heard; the young maids went back to the village at night. Jim, the gardener, could not possibly be reached; he had a small cabin of his own at quite a distance from the house.

Judy glanced over her shoulder, and it seemed to her the quantity and acrid odor of the smoke had increased. She smelled burning rubber, and now a fear she had not had time to realize before made her slightly sick. Rubber was insulation. If the wiring in the elevator burned, would the motor explode? What about the oil furnace? Was it anywhere near the elevator?

She turned back to the bed and saw that her efforts had at last borne fruit. Melissa had raised herself on one elbow, and she, too, was looking toward the elevator.

"Is there a fire in the elevator shaft?" she asked in an almost normal tone. "I suppose we'd better get downstairs. Just give me a minute to get awake. I took a sleeping pill . . . "

"There's no time for that," Judy said, her voice hoarse with panic. "Here's your robe. Put it on."

"Did you call Whitney?"

"No time for that either," Judy said, trying to keep her voice even. "Now do exactly as I say, Mrs. Beyer. Here's your cane. I will hold onto you until we get to the stairs . . . "

"I can't go downstairs," Melissa Beyer said. "I've been using the elevator for years. You go and call Whitney."

"I tell you there is no time. We've got to get out of this room — out of the house."

"Don't get frightened," Melissa admonished her nurse. "I'll try, if you think it's important, but I do insist we take my strongbox. It's right over there on the desk. And maybe you ought to get my mink coat out of the closet. Hadn't I better dress if we're going outside?"

Dear God, help me! Judy prayed to herself. Somehow I've got to make her see that every second we stay here brings us a little closer to death. Yet if I frighten her she won't be able to manage at all, and I can't carry her . . .

She put her arm around Melissa's waist and, summoning every ounce of control she possessed, said gently: "Now just walk with me. No need to be frightened, and no need to worry about your coat or papers. It's probably just a little fire. But I don't want you to inhale any more smoke."

Melissa Beyer attempted to pull away. "I believe you're hysterical, Judy. If you won't get the papers or my coat or call Whitney or do anything sensible, I'll have to do it all myself."

"You'll do as I tell you," Judy said, feeling her temper snap. "If you want to fuss around arguing with me and doing everything you can think of, I'll go and leave you here. You're too stubborn and wilful to be worth saving."

"Judy dear! The fire is really bad, isn't it? I didn't realize. Help me, Judy."

There was a sudden crash from somewhere downstairs, and a second later smoke poured out from under the elevator door. Judy, guiding her employer into the hall, did not identify the noise, but Melissa said at once:

"The elevator fell. The cable must have burned through."

All at once she began to tremble, not lightly but with a violent shaking that made it almost impossible for her to stand and that made her teeth chatter loudly. Judy, looking toward the stair well, knew despair. Somehow she had thought of the fire and smoke as confined to Melissa's room, but the hall below was filled with smoke, and the tiny red night light burning at the turn of the steps made it look as if they would descend into the inferno itself.

"Stay where you are a second," Judy choked. She ran into her bathroom and with trembling fingers picked a guest towel off the rack and soaked it in water. Then she dashed out and tied it swiftly around the older woman's nose and mouth. Melissa tried to speak but was shaken with spasmodic coughing. However, she was not trembling so violently, and she now limped docilely towards the head of the stairs.

"I'll stay two steps ahead of you,"

Judy told her, trying to keep from coughing herself. It suddenly occurred to her she had forgotten to turn off the water in the bathroom, and she almost laughed as she realized it was just as well if the water overflowed the basin. She told herself firmly she must not give way to panic.

They started down the stairs — those endless stairs — Judy two steps in the lead. She had her right hand on the banister, her left hand outstretched and her whole body braced in case Melissa should fall against her. In back of her she heard Melissa's labored breathing and the tap of her cane as she put it on the next step down and then dragged her leg down to meet it.

The stairs dropped away in the smoke. Judy's legs trembled and she was gasping for breath. She dared not look down for fear of pitching forward into the smoke-filled hall. Halfway down, she was aware all at once that she had not heard Melissa's cane. She turned and saw the older woman standing above her, still holding onto the banister but swaying uncertainly. In a second she had stepped back and put both arms tightly around her employer.

"Just a little bit more, Melissa. Please try. Don't give up now." Judy was almost sobbing. Melissa shook her head.

"Can't. Can't make it. You go. Let me sit down . . ."

Melissa's body suddenly sagged, a dead weight in Judy's arms. Although she was braced for it, Judy wondered for an instant if they would both go tumbling down the stairs. What could she do? How could she get out of this nightmare?

"Granny! Granny!"

"Here! Here we are, Whit!" Judy could not even be sure she had spoken, and she wondered if she had heard Whit's voice only in her imagination. Then she felt his strong arms touching her, his hands reaching out to grasp his grandmother's shoulders just above her own. His urgent voice was in her ear:

"Okay, Judy, you can let go now. I said, let go! I've got Granny; she won't fall. That's right, you hang on to the railing. Sit down on the step. I'll be right back."

The weight had gone. Judy felt the wood of the banister beneath her cramped fingers, and it was hot. She sank onto the step as Whit — only a bulky figure in the swirling smoke — picked up his grandmother and started carefully down the stairs. Judy sighed and relaxed. She mustn't let go of the banister. There was no feeling in her hand except for the burning sensation of hot wood. But she must not let go; somebody had told her — was it Whit? — to hang on. She must hang on. Nothing else mattered. How tired she was. If she could just go to sleep . . . go to sleep . . .

"Judy, Judy — my darling!"

It was Whit's voice. He sounded frightened, tender and loving all at once. Perhaps she had better not open her eyes. It was pleasant to lie there, breathing in air that was clear and sweet; her fingers touched soft wool. Perhaps it had been a nightmare after all and she was in bed dreaming. Suddenly, almost without volition, she sat up, her eyes wide.

"Melissa!" she cried. "Mrs. Beyer!" She broke off, coughing, looking at Whitney in a smoke-stained shirt, his face streaked with soot and his blond hair seeming lighter than ever before.

"Granny's all right now," Whit said soothingly. "Willard took her down to Greenmeadow House. He owns the place, you know, and Granny helped him get started. I'll take you down as soon as you can walk."

"I guess I passed out," Judy said, still choking.

"Yes," Whit said briefly. "But you remembered to hang on. I almost had to break your fingers to get them away from the banister. You're a brave girl, Judy."

Judy looked beyond him at the bulk

of the big house, still standing solid and foursquare against the darkened sky. Only fire was its enemy, Judy thought. Like a sickness, fire was gnawing away at the very vitals of the house. Smoke belched from every window, and ribbons of flame darted out and licked around the openings like voracious tongues. There was a faint sound of crackling and an occasional crash, but the sound was muffled as if it were far away.

"It doesn't make much noise," Whit said, as if reading her thoughts.

"No, death is not loud," Judy agreed. "And more than a house is dying now, Whit. We are watching the death of an era."

Whit looked at her sharply. "Don't you go fainting on me again. Do you think you can stand up now?"

Judy nodded and made the effort, although her legs still trembled. There were black-coated figures moving here and there; the volunteer fire department of Greenmeadow, she supposed, perhaps augmented by others from a nearby town. At any rate, she could see two streams of water pouring into the black openings that had been windows. But they seemed as totally ineffectual and inadequate as a trickle of water down a narrow mountain slope.

"Was anything saved?" Judy asked as she got into Whit's car.

"Only people," he said as he slid behind the wheel.

"I should mind my manners," Judy said finally. "Thank you for saving my life."

Whit turned the key in the ignition and looked down at her with a smile. "And thank you for saving Granny's life," he said with equal formality. "But we can discuss this at some other time; sometime when I can kiss you — after you've wiped off that smudge on your nose."

"You've got a smudge on *your* nose," Judy said demurely. "If I don't mind a smudge or two, why should you?"

15

THE TURRETS did not look very different from the time she had first seen it, Judy thought, as she got out of the car and stood looking up at the pile of masonry. At a quick glance, the outside walls seemed still intact, the copper-braced roof stood staunch, and although the gleam of the sun on broken windows spotlighted their forlorn look, there was not the complete devastation Judy had expected to see.

She walked slowly around the house until she stood facing the ill-fated fountain which now would never be installed. The Grecian maiden had been knocked from her pedestal and lay in pieces on the frozen ground. The cupids, however, still frolicked around the rim of the lower basin and held out their hands with the same engaging playfulness which the unknown sculptor had originally captured.

Judy looked toward the front door, but she had no intention of going in. She knew all the entrances would be blocked and that neither she nor other members of the household would be permitted to enter. The fire had finally died down early that morning, and the salvage crew had been in touch with Whit at Greenmeadow House.

Actually Judy did not know why she had come. The house held no memories for her, either fond or bitter. Yet its destruction marked the end of a definite period in her life, as it did for Melissa Beyer. Perhaps it was because of that sturdy woman she had come to stand here in the thin November sunshine. Melissa would never ask her to come, and she would never come herself. But surely it was up to Judy to make the visit without prodding and to carry back some word or some impression which might ease the pain Melissa Beyer must feel.

Her employer, however, had enjoyed an excellent unbroken sleep, once they were settled in their rooms at Greenmeadow House. Judy, tossing and turning on the twin bed next to her, had envied the elderly woman her ability to accept disaster and look forward to the future. She said as much to Melissa when the woman woke up that morning.

"My dear, when you have been as near death as I have been," Melissa said vigorously, "you learn to take everything else in stride. Even my disability, bad as it is, did not bring the world crashing about my ears. I was able to carry on then, and I am able to carry on now."

"You're pretty wonderful, did you know that?" Judy asked. "But what are you going to do now?"

"Right now I'm going to eat a hearty breakfast, and I suggest you go downstairs and see what arrangements Consuela has made about our food. I hope somebody has done something

245

about clothes, too. That yellow house-coat of yours is most becoming, my dear, but you can't run around Greenmeadow in it, and you'll find you'll have to do a lot of that."

After they had eaten breakfast, Judy had discovered Melissa's statement was accurate. She had had to attend to numerous errands, large and small. She had also found out Mrs. Beyer's at homes had been very worthwhile; they had cemented undying friendships, with the result that in this crisis there was such an eagerness to help and such tremendous sympathy for Melissa they were being drowned in kindness, to a point that was embarrassing.

Clothes poured in from everyone. Judy thought with amusement, as she tried on ski outfits, slacks, morning and afternoon dresses, sweaters, parkas and even a couple of fur jackets, that she had never had such a wardrobe in her life.

"I feel like a bride," she laughed

to Melissa, trying on a wool dress of winter white which Heindrich Shoen, on telegraphed instructions from his daughter Elsa and her roommate Bimi Dowling, had sent her by messenger.

"White is becoming to you," Melissa commented, "and I hope one day it will be a bridal outfit I see you wearing. Heindrich is an old fuddy-duddy in some ways, but he is kind. He sent me a hundred-dollar check and said I had won the wager we had on our next game of billiards. I had bet he couldn't touch me when next we faced each other across that table, and of course he's just making it an excuse to give me the money."

Melissa's old friends all sent gifts of various kinds, including jewelry and handkerchiefs and shoes. Melissa herself had to call a halt, finally. She asked her friend Willard, who owned the hotel — thanks to Mrs. Beyer, as Whit had explained — to put any other gifts that arrived into a special room. There they could be looked over later and appropriate thank-you notes written.

"You and I have got to have a talk, Judy," Mrs. Beyer said, settling herself in the rocking chair Willard had sent up to her suite. "You have seen me as a wilful old woman, intent on having her own way."

Judy made a negative gesture, but Melissa stopped her before she could speak.

"No, don't deny it, because I'm going right on being wilful. Whitney told me — it seems a long time ago, although it was only last night at dinner — that I couldn't dictate how the property was to be used, unless I was giving the place to some specific charity. You know?"

Judy nodded.

"Well, of course there was no sense asking Elaine to cooperate; I'm convinced her buyer was going to use The Turrets for some nefarious purpose. I was surprised to find Whitney was not only willing but anxious to have The Turrets used for some humane purpose. He's a fine young man, Judy," she broke off to say, "and I did so hope . . . " her voice trailed off momentarily, and then she said briskly: "How about Peter Baylis? Have you called and told him you were safe?"

"No," admitted Judy, "not yet."

"It's almost lunchtime," Melissa said. "Get him on the phone right now. He might hear about the fire and get terribly upset. I'll plug my ears if you want me to."

"No," said Judy, "it won't be that kind of phone call, Mrs. Beyer. I've promised Peter I would make a decision. But I've sort of hated to tell him. Anyway, I'll call him now."

It was eleven-thirty in the morning, and though Judy did not expect Peter to make any declarations of love, she was not quite prepared for the curt conversation which actually took place. First of all, she had a hard time convincing his secretary that her message was important, and finally said she would keep it brief and not hold up the conference which was apparently in progress.

Peter's greeting when he got on the phone was short. No, he had not heard about the fire. He was closeted with the two partners of his firm, and they had an important schedule to arrange before one o'clock; every moment counted. Judy, feeling rebuked, in her confusion repeated what she had already said. Although the fire had destroyed The Turrets, no one had been hurt, she stressed.

"That's good," said Peter, and then, apparently aware he was expressing too little concern, added more warmly: "Call me tonight, Judy. I'm really terribly busy right now. I'll have to hang up."

Judy's temper flared. Here she had been through a fire of major importance, and Peter hadn't an extra minute to hear about it! That decision she had been asked to make — she would tell him now, while he was in no mood to feel hurt or even interested.

"Just one more word, Peter," Judy said now. "I've decided."

"Decided?" Peter's puzzled voice came impatiently over the wire.

"You did ask me to marry you. At least I got that impression," said Judy. "I want to tell you I'm sorry, but the answer is no."

"What a time to start a discussion of marriage!" exclaimed Peter. "You are completely lacking in common sense, Judy. But I'd already guessed. You could have told me at a more convenient moment. But now that you *have* told me, I want to express my gratitude to you for not keeping me dangling any longer."

"That's the least I can do," said Judy sweetly: "let you off the hook."

"We'll still be friends," Peter began. "Yes, yes, I'll be there right away!" he called, apparently in answer to a summons from within the office. "Goodbye, Judy. I've got to rush."

Melissa Beyer was tactful enough not to refer to the conversation, although Judy knew from her eloquent expression she was aware what had taken place. Instead, speaking almost as briskly as Peter had done, the older woman outlined her plans for the future.

Once she had agreed to give the place away, she remarked, she had found a new freedom. Now she could do some of the things she had hardly known she wanted to do. For example, she thought of taking a convenient apartment — one close to New York. Consuela, who was getting no younger, would appreciate having fewer household cares. She herself would relish an occasional Broadway first night, she observed, and she could take in some of her favorite operas as well. Friends, even those living at a distance, would appreciate the chance to visit her and perhaps accompany her to concerts or the art galleries.

"I'm afraid I've allowed myself to get out of touch with many things I used to enjoy," she added.

Finally Judy asked where Whit had gone. She had been wondering and had hoped Melissa would tell her without being asked. But her employer was still enthralled with her own plans and was giving very little thought to the activities of anyone else.

"Oh, Whit went out early," she told Judy. "Consuela told me while you were down getting breakfast. First off, he had to go to the factory, of course, and from there I imagine he will drive over to the insurance office. We are fully covered, thank heaven, although I understand it will cost quite a little to tear down the walls, which are shaky, I suppose. Strange, isn't it — you can't even throw away or give away a part of your life without having it cost something in cash, as well as in emotional turmoil."

"I haven't said so before," Judy said, blinking back the tears, "but

I did want to tell you how brave I thought you were throughout this ordeal. It must be a frightful thing to face the loss of all you have treasured during a lifetime; you haven't even one memento except your memories to show for those years."

"The memories are enough," Melissa said, but her voice was suddenly husky. "I don't really know what I would have saved if I had had a chance. But it certainly wouldn't have been those old papers or that mink coat I was trying to get you to take. I never did like the coat, and I've had it for fifteen years. As for the papers, there's a copy of every one of them in my lawyer's safe."

"The cook in this hotel tells me Katy is going to Vermont to stay with an ailing sister," Judy said, deciding she had better change the subject.

"Yes," Melissa said contentedly. "Katy would have gone up there next spring in any event. I won't ask about your plans, my dear, but

I'd be grateful if you'd stay around for the next couple of weeks at least, until I get more or less settled. Right now I would suggest you take the car and run over to see how my godchild is coming along. Then get a breath of fresh air for yourself. You must be weary after all this excitement."

Judy had taken the car, but she had not driven to the hospital as Mrs. Beyer had suggested. The new mother needed rest more than anything else; a phone call had assured her both mother and child were doing fine. So she had driven around the countryside aimlessly, telling herself she was making plans for her own future. But in her heart she knew she was doing nothing of the sort. She simply did not want to think of the future at all.

How foolish can a girl get? she asked herself as she came out of a small lunchroom where she had ordered a cup of coffee and a sandwich, but left the sandwich untasted. I meet a man who is engaged to another girl. He takes me for a ride — two rides, but Mrs. Beyer demanded he do the honors the first time. Only the second ride counted — and that very little when you come right down to it. Oh, he said something romantic once, and I fell hopelessly in love with him with no more encouragement than that.

It is just as well, my girl, she told herself severely, that this whole situation is now resolved. No more hanging about hoping for a kind word from Whit Beyer! You will go back to New York, you will go back to work at Park View, and eventually you will forget there ever was such a place as The Turrets or Greenmeadow, or a blond young man whose very presence made you thrill to your fingertips — and all the way to the tips of your toes.

Having told herself off in such a fine manner, Judy had positively no excuse for stopping by the ruin of the house on her way back to the hotel. It was cold and windy and she shivered in the borrowed coat, not so much from the chill as from the desolation of the scene before here.

"I never expected to find you here," Whit's voice said behind her. "But I'm glad I did. I suppose you have been wondering about last night . . . "

"Just a kiss?" Judy laughed nervously. "I'm very grateful to you for taking my mind off the fire. I didn't think you felt an explanation was necessary."

"I'm not explaining why I kissed you," Whit said impatiently. "You're jumping to a few conclusions. I wanted to tell you about last night — before the fire. I went to see Elaine, you know."

"Your grandmother told me."

"Elaine admitted the man who was going to buy the property had been Jock's discovery, not hers. Or did you know that?" When Judy nodded, he went on: "I guess I've been a dope about Jock and Elaine. They really had something going for each other. But I couldn't see it."

"I don't know," Judy stammered. "Perhaps you are mistaken."

Whit laughed and there was genuine amusement in his voice. "No, I couldn't be mistaken. Elaine was packing when I went there last night. She was driving down to New York to meet Jock, and they were eloping to Virginia. I imagine they are already married."

"Oh. That's good, isn't it?" Judy said, looking at him questioningly. "Or do you feel hurt and rejected?"

"I don't feel anything except relief," Whit assured her. "I've discovered at last I never was in love with Elaine. I realize it was she who sold *me* on the idea, because she wanted to have some admirer around while waiting for Jock to succumb sufficiently to offer marriage."

"Maybe Peter feels nothing but relief, too," said Judy almost to herself. But Whit heard her.

"What about Peter?" he demanded. "Have you . . . "

"I told him I couldn't marry him,"

said Judy simply. "He didn't seem upset, so I thought perhaps he felt relief, too, the way you feel about Elaine . . . "

"You're shivering," said Whit suddenly. "We'd better get back to the hotel. Why did you come here, anyway?"

"It was just a thought." Judy's tone was rueful. "Your grandmother lost so much in the fire last night. She hasn't even a photograph or your grandfather's watch chain or any little personal memento of those she loved very much. It was silly of me, but I thought perhaps one of the firemen might have thrown something out of a window . . . It was just a foolish notion," she said, turning away from the house. "The place is an empty shell."

"It wasn't a foolish notion," Whit told her, and he sounded tender. Then he reached into his pocket and drew out something which he placed in her hand.

"Last night after I had taken you

to the hotel, I came back here. The fireman probing the ruins for valuables had found Granny's jewel box — but he didn't throw it out of the window. He gave it to me, and I'll give it to her. But I know that out of all the jewelry it contains, there's only one thing she'll really be overjoyed to receive — the locket and chain you have in your hand."

Judy pressed the catch, and the locket opened to reveal a picture of a young man in one of the halves and the picture of a pretty girl in bridal costume opposite.

"Granny always said she looked like you when she was your age," said Whit. "Doesn't this picture prove it?"

"In a way," returned Judy. "But this is the picture of a girl deeply in love, radiant with love."

"I would like to make you look as radiantly in love, Judy . . . Will you let me try? I was slow to find it out, but I can't live without your love, darling. Do you think that — in time — you could love *me* — enough to marry me?"

"Well, I don't know . . . " Judy paused, the mischievous dimple near her mouth provocatively deep.

"Please," Whit interrupted, "don't answer me now. Don't say what you're going to say . . . "

"Silly," said Judy. "All I was going to say is, I don't know how I could love you more than I do this minute, Whitney Beyer. I've loved you from the first minute I saw you, but I didn't find it out until — oh, until I felt as if I would die if I could never tell you. But I'm telling you now. Oh, Whit!"

"Oh, Judy!"

His arms were around her, his lips almost on hers.

"Your grandmother will be pleased," murmured Judy.

"Like grandmother, like grandson." Whit grinned and kissed her thoroughly.

"I think," said Judy, as he released her, but only within the circle of his arms, "I'm pleased, too."

"That makes it unanimous," said.
Whit.

THE END

WITH SOMEBODY ELSE
Theresa Charles

Rosamond sets off for Cornwall with Hugo to meet his family, blissfully unaware of the shocks in store for her.

A SUMMER FOR STRANGERS
Claire Hamilton

Because she had lost her job, her flat and she had no money, Tabitha agreed to pose as Adam's future wife although she believed the scheme to be deceitful and cruel.

VILLA OF SINGING WATER
Angela Petron

The disquieting incidents that occurred at the Vatican and the Colosseum did not trouble Jan at first, but then they became increasingly unpleasant and alarming.